The Dragon's world was about to come crashing down

The fat was in the fire, and blood debts long deferred were being called in.

The Dragon will devour you.

A prophecy, or mere bravado?

Mack Bolan couldn't say, and it wouldn't have changed his plans in either case. One dragon or another had been trying to devour him for years, without success. If he had let the fear of sudden death prevent him from continuing, his war would have been over on Day One.

That he had come this far was testament to the Executioner's courage and determination. What transpired within the next few hours would be a testament to his survival skills.

The Executioner was blitzing on, to Hell if necessary.

No maps were needed. He already knew the way.

MACK BOLAN ®

The Executioner

DON PENDLETON'S

EXECUTIONER®
THE
RIDE THE BEAST

THE RED DRAGON TRILOGY

BOOK III

A GOLD EAGLE BOOK FROM
WORLDWIDE®

TORONTO • NEW YORK • LONDON
AMSTERDAM • PARIS • SYDNEY • HAMBURG
STOCKHOLM • ATHENS • TOKYO • MILAN
MADRID • WARSAW • BUDAPEST • AUCKLAND

First edition August 1996
ISBN 0-373-64212-1

Special thanks and acknowledgment to
Mike Newton for his contribution to this work.

RIDE THE BEAST

Printed in U.S.A.

He who passively accepts evil is as much involved in it as he who helps to perpetrate it. He who accepts evil without protesting against it is really cooperating with it.

—Martin Luther King, Jr.

Simple protest doesn't always do the trick with evil in the flesh. Sometimes you need a more forceful approach—like going for the jugular. This is one of those times. No quarter, no prisoners.

—Mack Bolan

THE
MACK BOLAN®
LEGEND

Nothing less than a war could have fashioned the destiny of the man called Mack Bolan. Bolan earned the Executioner title in the jungle hell of Vietnam.

But this soldier also wore another name—Sergeant Mercy. He was so tagged because of the compassion he showed to wounded comrades-in-arms and Vietnamese civilians.

Mack Bolan's second tour of duty ended prematurely when he was given emergency leave to return home and bury his family, victims of the Mob. Then he declared a one-man war against the Mafia.

He confronted the Families head-on from coast to coast, and soon a hope of victory began to appear. But Bolan had broken society's every rule. That same society started gunning for this elusive warrior—to no avail.

So Bolan was offered amnesty to work within the system against terrorism. This time, as an employee of Uncle Sam, Bolan became Colonel John Phoenix. With a command center at Stony Man Farm in Virginia, he and his new allies—Able Team and Phoenix Force—waged relentless war on a new adversary: the KGB.

But when his one true love, April Rose, died at the hands of the Soviet terror machine, Bolan severed all ties with Establishment authority.

Now, after a lengthy lone-wolf struggle and much soul-searching, the Executioner has agreed to enter an "arm's-length" alliance with his government once more, reserving the right to pursue personal missions in his Everlasting War.

1

Bangkok, Thailand

The Patpong district of Bangkok has something for everyone. The city's original red-light district, it consists of four parallel streets. Patpong 1 and 2 are lined with girlie bars, where entertainment ranges from nude dancers to the "live shows" upstairs, with smiling "hostesses" available to any customer with time and inclination, plus the ready cash in hand. On Patpong 3, the clubs are mostly gay bars, with transvestite shows in place of dancing girls, while Patpong 4 is proud of its exclusive Japanese restaurants and massage parlors, highly selective in whom they admit.

With an estimated 500,000 of the city's female population presently employed in "entertainment-related activities," Bangkok has gained a reputation as the Brothel of the East—perhaps the Brothel of the World. It was a favored stop for GIs taking R & R from Vietnam, and modern package tours deliver some three million tourists yearly to the city, an estimated one-third of whom are drawn specifically by Bangkok's free and easy reputation. Prostitution, while illegal, is among the top-three money-making trades in Bangkok.

Mack Bolan's mind wasn't on sex as he approached the Happy Rabbit Club on Patpong 2. The muggy climate limited his options, as far as concealment of military hardware was concerned, so he had settled for a baggy shirt to

hide his shoulder holster and a floppy canvas shopping bag
to hold the mini-Uzi, plus the stun and smoke grenades.

There were too many customers for him to use fragmen-
tation grenades. A massacre of innocent civilians—even if
they came to Patpong with the most peculiar lusts to satisfy—wasn't on Bolan's menu for the evening. He was focused on the owners of the club, together with whatever
muscle they employed to guard the place and keep the customers in line.

He paid the cover charge of fifty baht—a blue note,
worth about two dollars—bracing for the smoke and noise
that met him as he crossed the threshold. He was intercepted by a smiling hostess in her teens who led him to a
table near the runway. By the time he took his seat, another girl was planted on the chair beside him, scooting
closer, one hand on his thigh.

"You like me, sir?"

"What's not to like?"

The girls on stage wore numbers to facilitate selection by
discriminating shoppers. Bolan bought a pair of watered
drinks, sipped his and watched the show, while his companion finished half of hers in one long swallow. She mis-
took his trousers for a napkin, wiping warm, damp fingers
on his inner thigh.

"You like to go upstairs?" she asked.

"Is that allowed?"

"Sometimes," she said smiling at him, "for special
friends."

"Why not?"

"I take your bag for you?"

"No, thanks. It's heavy."

"I got muscles. You just wait and see."

"I'm looking forward to it," the soldier replied.

Bolan's guide led him up to the second floor and was
veering toward a numbered bedroom when he stopped her,

caught her arm and let her see the Uzi submachine gun. She
tried to squirm away, but he held her fast.

"I need to see the boss. You follow that? Big man in
charge?"

"Down there!" Her free hand pointed to the far end of
the hallway, flanked by numbered doors on either side.

"Is he alone?"

She hesitated, finally shaking her head.

"How many guns?"

"All different, every night."

"We'll have to take our chances then."

She led the way reluctantly, with Bolan close behind her.
The bedrooms were mostly silent, though he heard a
woman giggling from one, the bedsprings squeaking from
another. They were almost to the private office when the
door swung open and a young Chinese man in a shiny suit
stepped out, as if to greet them. At a glance, he saw nothing unusual about the tall American accompanied by a
hooker, but an instant later he worked out where they were
headed. Bolan saw the flash of trouble in his eyes and
jerked the girl aside, his Uzi stuttering a 3-round burst before the gunner had a chance to reach his sidearm.

Impact blew the dead man backward through the open
doorway. Bolan palmed a stun grenade, released the pin
and lobbed the bomb after him. He fell back into a crouch
against the nearest wall and closed his eyes, palms pressed
against his ears. The flash-bang rocked him, even so, but he
was on his feet and moving in a heartbeat, closing in to
catch his enemies before they rallied and were able to defend themselves.

The office contained four men, and they squirmed and
wriggled on the floor like stranded fish, except for one who
had apparently collided head-on with a metal filing cabinet when the grenade went off. The others gasped or cursed
and tried to get their bearings, deafened by the blast and
blinded by a million-candlepower flash of light. When two

of the men spotted him in the doorway, they started to go for their hardware.

With short bursts from the Uzi, the Executioner worked the room from right to left, taking out the four of them in seconds flat.

And it was time to leave.

Downstairs, the blast and gunfire had been audible despite the constant throb of heavy-metal music. Two young soldiers met him on the stairs, guns drawn, but they were unclear on the nature of their mission, huddled close together when they should have been spread out to make things difficult for an opponent. Bolan hosed them with 9 mm parabellum slugs that punched them backward down the stairs. He lobbed a smoke grenade down past their crumpled bodies, then stepped across them as he joined the flow of frightened customers and B-girls making for the street.

Outside, the warm night closed around him like a sweaty fist. The glare of neon stained his face bright crimson as he put the Happy Rabbit Club behind him, moving toward another target.

Glancing at his hands in that harsh light, it seemed that they were stained with blood.

DAVID MCCARTER CROSSED Ratchawong Road on foot, westbound, to enter the heart of Chinatown, a trading center for Thailand's largest ethnic minority over the past two centuries. Few tourists lingered after nightfall in the district—there were no hotels for foreign visitors in Chinatown—but neither were the residents inclined to question strangers who appeared to know where they were going and proceeded without apparent fear.

But you took your chances on the streets of Bangkok, and Chinatown was no exception. When the three young men approached McCarter, two blocks from his destination, he wasn't inclined to argue or debate the issue. With a timetable to keep, he flicked the right side of his light-weight sport coat back and let them see the MP-5 K sub-machine on its swivel harness.

"Any questions?"

There were none. His would-be adversaries vanished down a pitch-black alley, and he waited for their footsteps to recede before continuing on his way. He had a date with several men who didn't even know that he existed, and the Phoenix Force commando meant to be on time.

There was no sex for sale in Bangkok's Chinatown. The Chinese working girls wound up in Patpong, or with out-call services that made deliveries to various hotels. The major drug deals, likewise, were conducted elsewhere, in the lavish suites of wealthy visitors or on the waterfront, along the Chao Phraya River. That wasn't to say that Chi-natown was without vice. Covert opium dens and quiet gambling clubs thrived, and the deadly syndicates—the Triads—based their operations for the entire nation there, with tentacles that spanned the Golden Triangle.

McCarter's first target that evening was a social club, the Da-chang Mei-qi, where he was informed that members of the Triad known as 14K convened when they had nothing else to do. Sometimes they brought in entertainment, but this night they'd have an unexpected floor show.

McCarter saw the social club ahead of him, walked past it, then turned left down a dirty, smelly alley where the vis-ibility was next to zero. Reaching underneath his jacket, he produced a six-inch dagger and held it with the blade pressed flat against his leg, prepared to strike without a moment's hesitation if he was confronted by an enemy. Moments later he entered a narrow street that ran behind the Triad social club.

It was the kind of place that locked its doors against in-truders, but relied upon the reputation of its owners in the place of burglar alarms. No sane Chinese would break into a building owned and operated by the 14K. It was unthinkable, an action tantamount to suicide.

McCarter tried the knob from force of habit, slipped his dagger back into its sheath, then went to work with steel picks on the lock. It took him all of sixty seconds, no great time in an emergency, but he preferred to do the job with no unnecessary noise. The Briton held the compact submachine gun ready as he stepped across the threshold, then softly closed the door behind him, shutting out the night.

He followed voices and the odor of tobacco to a kind of recreation room that featured mah-jongg tables and a wet bar, sofas and recliners, with a big-screen television in the corner. They were obviously plugged into a dish for satellite reception, picking up a game show out of Italy that featured women taking off their clothes as they competed for a suite of bedroom furniture. The dialogue was wasted on McCarter and his targets, but the voluptuous breasts on display kept their attention from the new arrival in the doorway.

Counting heads, he made it seven shooters, three of them with weapons showing. They were casual about it, nothing to suggest that they expected trouble. Packing guns was second nature to these men, like putting on their pants before they went out in the morning. It was much the same with him, McCarter thought, but the advantage of surprise had given him the winning hand this time.

Unless he blew it.

Thirty rounds for seven gunners meant that he would have to be precise—no wastage as he worked his way around the room, or he would have to stop and feed his SMG another magazine.

Starting on his left, McCarter hit the nearest Triad gunman with a three-round burst that knocked him sprawling from his easy chair. The racket brought them all around, heads snapping, bodies springing into motion, but he had the feel of it by then, and he was on a roll.

The next two had been playing mah-jongg when he shot their comrade, both men kicking back their chairs and bolting to their feet. They gave him better targets that way, and he spent nine rounds between them, dropping them in a heap that took the table down, as well.

A bullet seared the air beside McCarter's head and spoiled his timing, made him swivel to his right and face a Triad who was faster on the draw than his companions. He was lining up another shot, when parabellum manglers stitched a line of holes across his chest and hurled him backward, tumbling across the sofa where he had been seated moments earlier.

It went to hell from there, with three guns blasting at McCarter, while his adversaries cursed and raved in Cantonese. He tracked one runner, tagged him with a sweeping burst that plucked the man off his feet and slammed his face into the giant TV screen.

And that left two.

McCarter wasn't counting, but he knew the MP-5 K had to be close to empty. The two gunners were still fighting back as he sought cover in the shadow of a sofa with a dead man draped across it. Bullets smacked into the leather-covered cushions, twanging springs and splintering the sofa's heavy wooden frame.

Get moving!

It was guesswork, but he calculated that his adversaries would expect him on the left side of the sofa as he faced them, which would give him access to the open door, a chance to get away. Instead, he bolted to the right, slid out below their line of fire and caught them standing bunched together, breaking every rule of combat in close quarters. Holding down the trigger on his SMG, he started at their feet and cut a zigzag swath, thigh-high, before his magazine ran dry.

His enemies were down, but far from out. McCarter drew his Browning Hi-Power double-action semiauto pistol from its shoulder rig and rose to finish it. The wounded men were squirming, cursing, one of them still clinging to his weapon, while the other's piece had spun out of his reach when he went down. McCarter shot the armed man first, one round between the eyes, then turned and gave his friend another.

He was retreating toward the doorway, reaching underneath his jacket for a backup magazine to feed the SMG, when he heard footsteps in the corridor outside. McCarter finished loading in a rush and stepped back from the entrance to the rec room, waiting. Seconds later he was ready when a young Chinese peered in, beheld his fallen friends and stepped across the threshold with a dazed expression on his face.

McCarter waited three more heartbeats, but the new arrival appeared to be alone. "Bad timing," he announced, and watched the shooter stiffen, standing frozen with a shiny autoloader in his hand.

The gunner could drop it and survive to fight another day, or try his luck and die. McCarter knew there was no choice involved. The young man's sense of honor would demand some effort, even knowing it would cost his life. If he did nothing, threw the gun away, his honorable ancestors would be disgraced. Better to make the effort and retain some face, than to survive and be reviled as a pathetic coward by everyone he knew.

McCarter had the gunner covered when the man swung back to face him, tracking with the pistol. Five rounds at a range of six or seven feet was all it took to end another promising career and leave the soldier's flaccid body laid out with his comrades on the blood-slick vinyl floor.

The Briton spent another moment checking out the corridor and rooms beyond, alert for any new surprises that the social club might have to offer. There was only silence, though, and he was satisfied to let it go at that.

The squalid alley didn't smell as bad, as he backtracked to his car. For all the odors pent up in that little stretch of hell on earth, at least he didn't have to breathe the reek of sudden death. It was a sweet relief to clear his head, however briefly, while he moved on to the next appointment on his list.

More of the same. War everlasting, as his good friend often liked to say.

It was some way to live.

Some way to die.

IT TOOK THE BEST PART of an hour for the first shock waves to reach Lao Fan and tell him he was under siege. He was accustomed to disputes in Bangkok, where three different Triads operated trading centers, all involved with China white, and violence was a common circumstance.

This was different, though. Fan could tell that much from the ferocity of the attacks, their public nature and the fact that he had a survivor—barely—from the Happy Rabbit Club. When he came out of his delirium for moments at a time, the young man named his adversary as a round-eye, tall and dark. He could be mad, of course, but Fan didn't think so.

He had heard about the troubles suffered by his Triad brothers in the European territories, half a world away. More recently, there had been massive bloodletting in Burma. The red pole for Rangoon had been wiped out in that campaign, along with General Tuan Khoo, a major warlord in the Golden Triangle, supplier of a vast amount of opium and China white.

Fan had no idea of what the final damages would be in Burma, or what they would mean to him, as he continued doing business from Bangkok. Khoo would have successors waiting in the wings, unless his army was annihilated, and there had been no suggestion of disaster on that scale. The shipments from Khoo's district might be tardy for a while, but there were other sources in the Triangle that would take up the slack. Fan didn't believe in putting all his cobras in one basket, knowing as he did how they were prone to turn on one another, striking aimlessly, until you had a basket full of dead snakes on your hands.

Preparedness permitted Fan to avoid all sense of panic, even knowing that the raiders fresh from Burma—and, presumably, from Europe—were now in Bangkok, picking off his soldiers, angling for a chance to bring him down in bloody ruin.

It would be a long, hard search, though, if they sought for any weakness in Fan. He hadn't fought his way up from the streets of Singapore through frailty, and his reputation as a killer for the family had been confirmed at least two dozen times before he reached the age of twenty-one. These days, of course, he rarely had to pull a trigger for himself, but he hadn't forgotten how.

In fact, if his intelligence department could identify the round-eyed enemies in time, it would be pleasant for Fan to lead the final push against them, see the dazed look on their pallid Western faces when he held a pistol to their heads and blew their brains out.

It was a miracle they had survived this long. They had to have some kind of backing from a sponsor hidden well behind the scenes. Fan wasn't concerned about that aspect of the problem. It would be Edward Wong's task to consider who had launched the global war, and why.

Fan had already spoken to his hill chief in Hong Kong. It troubled Wong to hear that violence was continuing in Asia, drawing closer to his own headquarters day by day. Fan made a note of the apparent tremor in Wong's voice as he was speaking, filed the information for future reference, just in case he ever felt the need to test Wong's mettle, maybe challenge him for leadership of the 14K.

Meanwhile, Fan thought, he should be speaking to his mainland counterpart. Xiao Kong wasn't a soldier, even though he wore a military title—Colonel Kong, *Comrade* Colonel Kong. It made Fan laugh, but never where the mainlander could hear him. The elaborate merger of the 14K and mainland Communists had been devised, so he was told, as a matter of mutual benefit. Hong Kong reverted to Beijing's control in one more year, but the regime in power had been drifting westward for a long time now, accepting bits and pieces of the capitalist culture, leaning toward some semblance of a free-market economy. There was already plenty of corruption in Beijing and in the provinces. Fan would feel at home discussing business with the spokesmen of the vaunted People's Revolution.

They were just like him, but terrified to recognize that basic truth.

The call to Kong could wait. Just now, Fan needed to communicate with his commanders in the field, prepare them for a kind of war that would be new to them.

Still, it was good to learn new things. It kept a body fresh.

And there would be enough stale bodies in Bangkok before the fight was finished. Lao Fan had no doubt of that.

No doubt at all.

YAKOV KATZENELENBOGEN parked his rental car on Chakraphet, near the canal, and locked it, following the course of muddy water fifty yards or so on foot to reach the Chao Phraya waterfront. The river kept Bangkok connected to the nearby Gulf of Thailand, where commercial liners, fishing boats and private pleasure craft all jockeyed for position, any one of them potentially a carrier for contraband departing Thailand, bound for parts unknown.

Most of the contraband shipped out of Bangkok would be China white or uncut opium, but there was also an increasing trade in human flesh. Some of those travelers without documents were Chinese refugees who pawned their futures, fleeing as indentured servants to a "better life" in Europe, Canada or the United States—where they would live in fear of Immigration and the Triads, wondering which heavy hand would fall upon their shoulders first. If there were ChiCom spies and saboteurs among them, they were well rehearsed, prepared to hide in place for months or years before the signal came to carry out specific orders.

There were other covert travelers from Bangkok, too, but they didn't depart the country willingly. Those were the sex slaves, children and young women purchased from their families in the countryside, sometimes abducted from the slums of Bangkok, to be sold like livestock in the flesh marts of the Middle East, Africa, South America and Europe. Slavery didn't lay a glove on heroin where profits were concerned, but it was still a multimillion-dollar industry for those who had the nerve, the contacts and the deficit of common decency required to trade in human beings.

Katzenelenbogen saw the warehouse up ahead, the Giu-pai Jiao-tong. He knew part of it meant "transport company," and felt less than burning curiosity about the rest. It was enough for him to recognize the target, know the kind of men involved, and some of what went on behind those corrugated metal walls—enough to make Katz risk his life in bringing them to grief.

Three cars out front told Katz the place wasn't deserted. Mounting concrete steps to reach the loading dock, he drew the mini-Uzi from underneath his baggy tourist's shirt and thumbed off the safety. The metal access door stood open, with a wooden wedge in place to hold it there. Considering the temperature and cost of air-conditioning in Bangkok, Katz suspected it was a pathetic compromise to keep the warehouse from becoming one gigantic oven.

By the time he cleared the small, empty reception area, he was already sweating through his shirt and khaki pants. The weather seemed to drain him, made him wish that he could leap headfirst into a swimming pool, or simply lie down in the shade somewhere with six or seven frosty beers to cool him off.

Better luck next time.

His targets—four of them, at least—were gathered in the office someone had constructed out of plywood and drywall, a smallish cubicle that fronted on the warehouse proper. In the main room of the yawning barn, perhaps two dozen girls and women sat together in a circle, facing outward, as if in a defensive posture chosen to repel attack.

Too late, Katz thought, considering the fact that they were trapped already.

Three more Chinese, armed with automatic rifles, were positioned for triangulated fire around the clutch of helpless hostages. The flesh peddlers in the office were debating price, or maybe details of delivery. Katz counted two Chinese and two who looked like Arabs, though he couldn't begin to guess their nationality.

To hell with details.

He was fuming now, but understood that everything would have to go like clockwork once he opened up the Pandora's box. The gunners were his danger point, but he couldn't take all of them at once, the way they were positioned. An effort to attack them from a distance, leaving four guns in the office, would have been ill-advised to say the least.

He tugged a frag grenade from the pocket of his slacks, released the pin and lobbed the bomb through the open portal of the office. It bounced off one Arab's head and landed on the desk, with three men peering down at it, the other in pain, with one hand clasped against his aching skull.

Three seconds.

Four.

It blew before they could react, and Katz ducked to avoid the shrapnel, swiveling to bring the Triad gunners under fire before they could assimilate the grisly evidence of carnage in the office. On his left, the nearest one was easy, standing with his rifle and his guard down. The parabellum shockers cut his legs from under him and slammed him facedown on the concrete floor, blood pooling rapidly beneath his corpse.

The other two were scrambling for their lives, no more thought for orders or their duty than a cornered rat might have for dining etiquette. One fired an aimless burst in Katzenelenbogen's general direction, then broke toward the nearest exit, while number three was busy scrambling up a stack of wooden packing crates in search of altitude.

Katz tracked the runner, leading him enough to make it stick when he squeezed off a 3-round burst and spun his target like a dervish, bringing him down with jarring force. The gunner lost his rifle, saw it spin away, but he was in no shape to chase it, crimson soaking through his pale blue shirt from several deadly hits.

And that left one.

The prisoners were finally tuned in to what was happening, a number of them crawling rapidly away on hands and knees, while others struggled to their feet. Above them, on his perch of packing crates, their sole surviving watchdog couldn't seem to make his mind up whether he should try to stop the exodus of female slaves or work on nailing down the stranger who had killed his comrades on the floor below.

He compromised at last, with a short burst toward the prisoners that knocked two women sprawling, dead or dying where they lay, then he turned his gun on Katz. By that time the Israeli had his target in the mini-Uzi's sights. He held down the submachine gun's trigger down and sprayed his target with the remainder of his magazine, some twenty parabellum rounds unloading in perhaps a second and a half. He never knew how many found their target, but enough struck home to punch the shooter through a jerky little dance atop his perch before momentum and gravity took over and he plummeted to earth.

All done.

Some of the girls and women had already disappeared, while others stood and gaped at Katz, as if expecting him to fire on them, now that the men were dead. He knew perhaps a dozen words in Thai, gleaned from a phrase book on the flight in from Rangoon, and he was bound to mispronounce whatever he attempted. Even so, he felt the need to utter *some* words in the midst of so much death and suffering.

And what he came up with was *"Chok-dee-kup,"* a phrase that seemingly did double duty, serving both as "good luck" and "goodbye." Katz let it stand for both and left them where they were, retreating toward the exit on the loading dock. When he had cleared the scene, there would be time enough to find a public telephone and try to make the local lawmen understand where they should go, what they should do.

The cops and hostages would all be on their own from there.

Katz had a hit list of his own to work through, and his time was running short.

2

Reid Delaney wondered, sometimes, whom he had insulted back at Langley to receive the Bangkok posting. The duty had its ups and downs, as Carricker would say—*did* say, with nagging regularity— but after three years on the job, the Patpong scene had lost its mystery, the first allure that sucked a young man in and made him wonder if he'd died and gone to someplace very different than the heaven he had learned about in Sunday school.

But that was playtime, and the thing that really got him down these days in Bangkok was the job. He understood the Company's position and agreed with it in principle: the cold war wasn't really over, it had merely shifted theaters. The Red Chinese were little changed, despite their lust for blue jeans and Big Macs, from when they sent their troops across the Yalu River to assault MacArthur's spearhead back in 1951. The party leaders ruled by fist and by fear, in spite of "cultural exchanges" and sporadic trade agreements with the West. Dissenters still caught hell for opening their mouths in public, and United Nations resolutions condemning the state of human rights in mainland China were normally defeated, with the new "enlightened" Russians voting to give Beijing a break. The truth about China, Delaney realized, was more apparent on the bloodstained pavement of Tiananmen Square than in the antics of a table-tennis team.

And his concerns weren't restricted to the Red Chinese, by any means. Their shadow dominated Southeast Asia, but the Triads were another major problem, not to mention terrorism—left- or right-wing, take your pick—and half-baked revolutionary schemes that simmered in the slums of every Asian land from Pakistan on through the Philippines. You had the drug trade—dominated by the Triads and the Yakuza—along with those persistent, if elusive, tales of slavery. Gunrunners, pirates, warlords—all behaved as if they were living in the seventeenth century, instead of creeping up on the twenty-first.

All that to cope with, and, incredibly, his job still came out boring, six days out of seven. He shuffled paperwork and filed dull reports in triplicate, the typing interspersed with meals or trips to nudie bars, where he debriefed his contacts, crossed their palms with silver and collected information in return.

Not that his information ever came to anything, of course. Three years in Bangkok, and Delaney couldn't think of one occasion when his bulletins had led to any concrete action in the field. They were "reviewed" and "analyzed" at Langley, bureaucratic euphemisms meaning someone glanced at them and stuck them in a filing cabinet, out of sight and out of mind.

Until today.

Delaney didn't know for sure if he could take the credit for the latest action in Bangkok, but there was something happening, regardless. Strangers had arrived in the city from America, and he was on his way to meet one of them. From what he gathered, they were covert action boys, the kind who earned their paychecks kicking ass and taking names. Some Triad asses had been kicked already, in Patpong and Chinatown, and while Delaney didn't have a righteous clue to what was happening, it got his blood up, all the same.

Dammit, *this* was why he joined the Company straight out of Yale. James Bond. "I Spy." "The Man From U.N.C.L.E." Never mind that those were hokey pulp adventures, more sci-fi than down-to-earth intelligence. Delaney wanted action, and he hadn't seen it yet, in seven years of playing secret agent for the home team in Virginia.

Maybe this time.

He was strolling toward a small café on Silom Road, not far from Patpong, highly conscious of the Smith & Wesson automatic in its shoulder holster, chafing at his shoulders, giving him a charley horse below one shoulder blade. He almost never wore the gun, knew it was risky going armed in Thailand, even with his diplomatic passport, but the way things had been heating up in Bangkok, he would rather be prepared than let the bastards catch him with his pants down. As for actually shooting someone, he would have to think about that for a while. It would depend upon the situation, certainly, and whether he—

Delaney's reverie was interrupted as he reached his destination, paused outside to get his tie and jacket squared away and make sure the pistol wasn't hanging out where everyone could see.

He swallowed hard and stepped inside the restaurant to meet his fate.

IT CAME AS NO SURPRISE to Xiao Kong that the Americans would try to sabotage his country's master plan. He had considered British intervention, briefly, when the first reports of round-eyed saboteurs had been relayed from North America and Europe, but it struck him that the Britons didn't have nerve enough to operate that way in the United

States, nor probably in London, when it came to that. The sun had long descended on their global empire, and the SIS—or MI-6, depending on the jargon of the day—didn't possess the kind of men required for waging urban war without regard to niceties of law. Their epic stalemate with the IRA had proved that point beyond a shadow of a doubt, and once a nation lost its nerve, its teeth, the rest was all downhill.

As for the brash Americans, they couldn't make their minds up as to whether they preferred John Wayne or Alan Alda as a role model for dealing with the world at large. Their President was fond of "reasoning" with trouble-makers, couching threats in "diplomatic" terms, but all he did was wind up looking weak and spineless. On the other hand, it was a fact well-known to covert operators in Beijing and elsewhere that America could still lash out with furious, destructive power when provoked beyond the limits of her tolerance. Saddam Hussein had learned that lesson—for a time, at least, before his childish arrogance began to reassert itself—and there had been a hundred other, lesser-known examples during recent years. A raid across the border here, a sniper's bullet there, a bomb blast somewhere else . . . the word got back to those who understood what they were looking for.

America wasn't a toothless paper tiger yet, whatever copywriters in Beijing were fond of saying in their editorials. A clumsy giant was more like it, slow and ponderous at times, not always quick or clear of mind, but lethal in a clinch.

Even a drowsy giant could be dangerous, just rolling over in his sleep.

Kong had always been a cautious man. He understood the danger of the Dragon's dealings with the 14K, but it had paid rich dividends so far, and there were great days coming, if they kept their wits about them, taking full advantage of each golden opportunity. The raids in Europe and Burma were a setback, granted, but it didn't mean their effort was doomed to failure. Kong wouldn't believe it was too late to salvage order out of chaos and preserve the Dragon's plan.

If he could stop their enemies in Bangkok, how much more impressive would it be than if he begged for help or hid himself from danger, waiting for the storm to pass? Kong had military training, knew enough of strategy to understand that it was critical for him to capture the initiative and hold it, even as his enemies were trying to unnerve him with their hit-and-run techniques. He could expect cooperation from Lao Fan, and that meant much in Bangkok, where the 14K had better than five hundred soldiers armed and ready to defend their trade in drugs and human flesh.

Kong privately regarded Fan and his gangsters with contempt, but this was business, mixed with politics, and he would swallow his disgust at being forced to deal with animals in human form. Their tactics, when he thought about it, were no worse than those employed by the police at home when dealing with political dissenters. Any major difference lay in motive: Kong fighting for the People's Revolution, while his Triad allies of the moment were concerned with money—power on a local scale that let them terrorize pathetic peasant families and made them feel like men.

Kong thought he understood the Dragon's master plan, though it had never been explicitly laid out for him. When Fan and the Triads had performed their service to the state, there would be ample time to round them up and deal with them as the degenerates they were, eradicate them to the last man, so that only memories of their existence lingered.

How pleasant that would be, the last phase in a grand world strategy that would refute the lie of communism's "failure." It was Russia's failure, Kong told himself, predestined by corruption in the Kremlin, weakness and degeneracy in the men who ruled the party from their offices in Moscow. They had lost their focus, grown to love the luxuries that came with rank, and so had doomed themselves—their nation—to the spectacle of civil war and chaos, running off to the Americans with hats in hand to beg for foreign aid.

His masters in Beijing would never bow to such humiliating failure. They would die first, and ignite a conflagration that would purge the world of capitalist running dogs.

But, Kong decided, it would be much better to succeed—and to survive. He planned on it, in fact, but it would take some work, with unknown enemies already in Bangkok, attempting to destroy all he had worked for in the past two years.

Still, he wasn't afraid of work—or fighting, either, if it came to that. It wouldn't hurt to wash his hands in blood, might even make him stronger in the end.

Xiao Kong prepared himself for war.

"The name's Belasko," Bolan stated as he settled in the chair across from the young man and shook his hand.

"Delaney, Reid. You got a first name?"

"Mike."

"So," Delaney said, "what can I do you for?"

"Is this the place to talk about it?" Bolan asked.

"Good as any. We could go outside and walk around the streets, but if you're hot, we'd have to think about directionals. Same thing if we go cruising in a cab. You have a car?"

"About a block from here."

"If anyone was waiting for you, chances are it's wired."

In fact, it wasn't, but his point was clear.

"Okay," Bolan said. "Anyway, it's your neck if somebody listens in and doesn't like the program."

"That's the spirit. Lay it out."

"Long story short," Bolan said, "there's a merger going on between the 14K and certain ChiCom elements that specialize in causing problems for the world at large. We've been detailed to toss a wrench in where we can."

"Who's 'we'?" Delaney asked.

"That's need to know. You don't."

"Okay, let's try it this way—where do I come in?"

"Support through on-site field intelligence. I'm told you know the players—Triad members and associates, ChiCom illegals, who's straight-arrow on the cops and who's got a retirement plan in place with fat donations from his local narcodealer."

"These are things that come to my attention, now and then. The 14K, you said?"

"That's right."

"Their local red pole is Lao Fan. Some piece of work, but I guess you know that, right? Past couple years, he spends a lot of time with this guy Xiao Kong. He's supposedly some third-string player from the cultural attaché's office, but I didn't buy it when he first showed up in Bangkok, and I sure as hell don't buy it now."

"They see each other publicly?" Bolan asked.

"If you want to call it that," Delaney said. "These days, they meet for lunch or dinner maybe twice a month. We log a lot of phone calls back and forth, but always scrambled. Sometimes we confirm the numbers, but it doesn't tell us much. I couldn't give you much, in terms of evidence."

"I don't need evidence," Bolan told him.

"So, it's that way." Was that sudden sparkle in Delaney's eyes a glint of apprehension, or excitement? "You've already started, right? I mean, the Happy Rabbit and their hangout, down in Chinatown."

"You ask a lot of questions," Bolan said.

"How else am I supposed to learn?"

"You're not. This isn't Langley, and we're not engaged in some field exercise to let you work on theoreticals. This *is* the field, and people die sometimes. I'd like to keep as many of them as I can on the opposing side."

"Sounds like a plan."

"I'm hoping you can amplify our range of targets—names, addresses, homes away from home. Surprise is just about our only edge against the numbers."

"May I ask how many—"

"No."

"I get ya."

"What I need from you," Bolan said, "is a list of players, where they can be found at any given time of day. Whatever comes to mind that might be useful."

Delaney smiled. "Would that include a link between Xiao Kong and some left-wing guerrillas who've been tearing up the countryside the past eleven months or so?"

"I wouldn't be surprised."

"Okay. The front man is Chuan Sukreepirom, a native Thai, but when he talks, it's like you're listening to Chairman Mao, or maybe Ho Chi Minh."

"Indoctrinated?"

"Up the old wazoo," Delaney said. "His people seem to like him, though, and he's been winning converts in the villages. He's not hot stuff in Bangkok yet, but he's got feelers out, some people here in town who try and spread the word around. Just give him time."

"That's one thing I don't have."

"Maybe just as well," Delaney said. "I have a feeling this guy could be dangerous."

The CIA agent produced a pen and notebook, starting to write furiously as he talked about some recent actions the left-wing guerrillas had promoted. It was mostly small stuff—sniping soldiers in the hinterlands and setting bombs in smaller villages that failed to pay the "liberation army tax"—but it had a familiar ring to anyone with memories of Laos, Cambodia and Vietnam.

"You said he's got some people here in Bangkok?"

"Yes, indeed. Front men for propaganda, plus an action cadre. Nothing he'd like better than to move his war in town, the way it looks to me. Get some publicity, you know? The way I read this guy, he's getting tired of playing Robin Hood out in the boonies, everyone ignoring him except the troops they send out there to kick his ass."

"He's got Chinese support?"

"Most of his weapons," Delaney said, "plus any cash he can't beg, borrow or steal from the locals. If Kong's people cut him off tomorrow, he'd be operating on a shoestring."

"But he doesn't trust them?"

"Hey, would you? If Chuan's got any brains at all, he has to know they're moving him around the chessboard like your basic pawn. Smart money says he doesn't like it, but he has to pucker up and play the game unless he wants to kill the golden goose."

The list was finished, and Delaney passed it over, pocketing his ballpoint pen. Names and addresses filled the notebook page from top to bottom in tidy columns, adversaries marked for death.

"You've got Chuan's people on here?"

"Last four names," Delaney said. "You understand, the addresses are flexible, and then some."

"Roger that." He reached the bottom of the list and frowned. "And these coordinates, outside Khon Kaen?"

"That's Chuan himself...or was, the last time we were able to confirm from satellite surveillance. I should tell you, though, in case somebody plans on dropping by to sell him magazines, he keeps about two hundred men around his base camp all the time."

"That's good to know." The list went in his pocket, and Bolan offered Delaney his hand. "It's been a help. I'm hoping we don't have to meet again."

"You mean it's over, just like that?"

"It's barely started," Bolan told him, "but you want to keep away from this one, I can promise you."

"You may be right," Delaney answered, "but I'll keep my ears on, all the same. You have my number, right?"

"Affirmative."

"Don't hesitate to use it if you come up short."

"Okay."

He left Delaney sitting there and didn't look back. The young man was a veteran of the dirty, silent struggle that went on from day to day in Bangkok, but that silence was about to shatter, with a vengeance. Bolan didn't want Delaney on his conscience when the smoke cleared, and he hoped the spook had sense enough to keep his distance from the killing ground. If not, then it would be Delaney's problem.

The Executioner had troubles of his own—like getting out of Thailand with his Phoenix allies in one piece.

"LOOKS LIKE THE PLACE," McCarter said to Yakov Katzenelenbogen, while the gruff Israeli double-checked his target list.

"It's right," Katz told him, pocketing the crumpled slip of paper as he spoke.

They had agreed to hit the gambling house together, front and back, to minimize the risk and lay as much hurt on the Triads as they could in record time.

Casino gambling—like the thriving prostitution racket— was illegal in Bangkok, a fact that didn't slow the operators a bit. This club, on Nua Road, was small by Vegas standards, but it could accommodate two hundred players in the main casino, with some rooms upstairs for "special" games and entertainment, if the mood and price were right. Lao Fan was the proprietor—in fact, if not on paper—and the club made an inviting target as they started turning up the heat around Bangkok.

"You want the back?" Katz asked.

"Suits me," McCarter said.

"Two minutes?"

"Fine."

The Briton left the car and crossed the street, one eye on traffic, while he kept the other peeled for lookouts.

He motored down a side street and turned left into the alley that would bring him to the back door of the club, keeping one hand inside his blazer, cradling the stubby MP-5 K submachine gun on its swivel rig. He reached the door in time to meet a man in an apron taking out the trash. A quick glimpse of McCarter's weapon, and the guy took off without an argument, the door ajar as he had left it coming out.

McCarter checked his watch and waited on the step for thirty seconds more to give Katz all the time they had agreed upon. He crossed the threshold, moving toward the main casino, and counted four cooks sweating over woks and vats of frying oil.

Katz should be close by now, if not already in the clubhouse. It was time. McCarter swung his weapon from under cover and held it ready as he closed on the casino, following the noises that were so alike, no matter where you heard them: Bangkok, Monte Carlo or Atlantic City. Losing money was the kind of pastime that demanded gaiety, a who-cares attitude assisted by large quantities of alcohol and the proximity of people who feigned interest in your every word, regardless of the language you were speaking.

He was almost there when two young Triad hardmen stepped into the corridor, ten feet in front of him. They were emerging from the men's room, joking with each other, when the first one spied McCarter staring at them and elbowed his companion. Under the circumstances, they could either run or stand and fight.

They didn't run.

McCarter squeezed the MP-5 K's trigger when they started grabbing for their side arms, stitching them with a burst that dumped them over backward onto the floor. His weapon had no silencer, and it was loud enough to momentarily suppress all noise from the nearby casino. When the voices started up again, their jocularity had vanished. Someone screamed, and he heard men shouting angry, frightened questions, some of them in English, some in Thai and some in Cantonese.

The Phoenix Force commando stepped across his kills, proceeding toward the scene of chaos as a second automatic weapon opened up. That would be Katz, or someone firing at him, since they hadn't seen McCarter yet, and no wild bullets came his way. He picked up his pace up and reached the killing floor five seconds later.

Katz was in the main foyer, pinned down by half a dozen Triad gunners firing at him from a semicircular perimeter. Two others, stretched out on the floor in pools of blood, hadn't been quick enough to save themselves. Katz was returning fire, thereby encouraging the customers to turn and head out through the back.

McCarter leaped aside to let them pass, his focus on the gunners who were pumping angry rounds toward Katz. The nearest of them showed his profile to the Briton, rising from his crouch behind a table as he aimed his pistol with both hands. McCarter shot him in the side and dropped him where he stood, the sound of gunfire at their backs reminding others on the home team that the first shots heard that night hadn't come from the foyer, where Katz held his ground.

Another pair of gunners spun to face McCarter, but the effort was too little and too late. He nailed the man on his left with three rounds to the chest, kept turning in the same smooth motion, tagging number three while he was lining up his shot. The dying gunner vaulted backward, sprawled across a card table, but it hadn't been built to bear his weight and it collapsed beneath him with a crash.

Katz chose that moment to emerge from cover, while the three surviving hardmen were deciding which way they should turn and fire to maximize their chances for survival. Either way was hopeless now, with automatic weapons raking them from both sides, ventilated bodies jerking through a spastic dance of death before they crumpled to the floor.

The paying customers, meanwhile, had mostly cleared the premises, a pair of tipsy Germans bringing up the rear, rebounding from the walls and from each other as they ran. McCarter wished them well and turned to Katz, finding the Israeli on his feet, apparently unscathed.

"We finished here?" he asked.

"Almost," Katz said as he produced a fat incendiary canister from underneath his jacket.

"Right."

McCarter made a beeline for the front door, passing Katz as his companion made the pitch. Both Phoenix Force warriors were outside and moving toward their car when white smoke started leaking from the front door of the gambling club. A few more minutes with the thermite cooking, and the place would be a total loss.

"Are you all right?" McCarter asked his friend when they were rolling.

"Fine." Katz didn't sound it, but McCarter knew enough to keep from pushing.

Nerves could hit you anytime, most often when you least expected it. They were a price of living in the hellgrounds, dealing death and coming out the other side intact.

This time, at least.

"The night's still young," he said to Katz.

The gruff Israeli forced a smile. "I'm game, if you are."

"Check in with Striker first?"

"Why not? He may have something special for us by this time."

McCarter glanced at Katz again and found him staring out the window with a grim expression on his face, as if the hectic street scene had some special meaning for him, like an omen.

Forget it.

They had work to do, and time was always short, no matter how he tried to stretch it out. You never had enough to cover everything.

So they would check with Striker for a little something special. Death with all the trimmings, maybe, on a warm night in the Orient.

3

Khon Kaen

It was decided they should give Bangkok a breather, get out in the countryside and see what Chuan Sukreepirom was up to with his private army. A phone call to Reid Delaney at the U.S. Embassy arranged their charter flight. They wound up with a forty-something gap-toothed pilot who had probably been running contraband of one kind or another since he learned to fly and scraped up the money to get a plane—perhaps the very plane that took them north, Bolan thought, judging from the patchwork on the fuselage and wings.

They made it all the same, and it was getting on toward afternoon before they found a jeep to rent, stowed their equipment and began to drive in a southwesterly direction. Twice they stopped to see if they were being followed, killing time, aware that they would have to stash the wheels before much longer and proceed to Sukreepirom's compound on foot.

Dusk painted pastels on the sky before they got there, but they still had light enough to scout the layout, do a hasty head count and decide that the guerrilla leader had more like ninety soldiers in his camp, a break from the 150 they had been expecting.

They used the last part of daylight spotting landmarks in the camp: the CP tent, communications, motor pool, the

ammo dump. The camp was screened by camouflage netting to avoid detection from the air, but it retained the look
of something that could be torn down and reassembled in
a flash, if they were forced to run.

Some life, Bolan thought, hiding in a jungle clearing,
eating monkey and iguana when the staples ran out, alert
to every sound in case it meant the enemy was coming,
tightening the noose. Some great crusade this was.

He had run some hasty background on the group that
called itself Free Thailand, and he knew its members had
been linked to terrorist attacks from Udon Thani down the
length of the peninsula. Around two hundred dead, so far,
not counting rebels shot by the authorities in half a dozen
jungle skirmishes. It didn't sound like much compared to
Beirut or Colombia, but several recent incidents in Bangkok proper indicated that Sukreepirom's troops were
branching out. The "people's army" was abandoning its
rural base, at least in part, to look for fame and fortune in
the city.

If they were allowed to get that far.

By full dark, Bolan was in place, his comrades spotted
west and south of him on the perimeter. Three men couldn't
surround a camp that size, but they could use a combination of audacity and stealth to keep their enemies from
knowing they were only three. Once they had rung the dinner bell, they might just spark a feeding frenzy in the camp,
and anything could happen then.

The tall man lay in ferns and grass, peering down the
barrel of his Chinese-made AK-47, watching a meager
member of sentries walk their beats on the perimeter. It all
came down to manpower, and Chuan Sukreepirom apparently had no great fear of being taken by surprise at night.

So much the better.

Bolan checked his watch and saw that he had ninety seconds before the hellstorm started blowing. He, in fact, had
drawn the honor of beginning the festivities.

A sentry stopped to light a cigarette. A sergeant of the guard should have been standing by to slap it from his mouth and scorch his ears with hot invective, try to keep the young man alive a little longer.

Too late.

The Executioner already had him spotted, framed by rifle sights.

And it was time to rock and roll.

DAVID MCCARTER WAS READY and waiting when the first shots rattled off across the compound. He had worked his way in close, believing he had the sentries figured out, their timing. He could penetrate the camp if he was ready when the shooting started. All he needed was a small break, lookouts turning toward the sound of Bolan's rifle fire. If someone actually left his post to check it out, so much the better.

Now he saw his opening and seized it, charging from the shadows, sliding into cover near the south wall of the mess tent, crouching with his rifle braced across his knees. When no one challenged him, he slit the tent flap with his Ka-bar fighting knife and slipped inside.

The setup was like every other field mess he had seen in military service—minor variations in equipment, but the basic layout never changed. There was a stove and an oven, each with fuel tanks, and a row of coffee urns that looked like decompression chambers for a group of very short deep-sea divers. Furniture inside the tent had been kept to a minimum, and that was fine. McCarter had already found exactly what he needed.

From the heavy satchel slung across his shoulder, he removed a plastic-explosive charge, the detonator mounted but deactivated. In another heartbeat it was live and ticking, with the timer set for sixty seconds and molded to the smooth side of the propane tank that fed the stove.

McCarter left the tent as he had entered, through the makeshift exit he had opened for himself. The camp was going crazy now, with automatic weapons stuttering, muzzle-flashes winking in the night like fireflies in some frantic mating ritual.

But there was no life here, no procreation in the works. The game was death, and he had come to play for keeps.

The Phoenix Force commando struck off for the ammo dump, expecting opposition when he got there. Taking out the enemy's supply of ammunition and explosives would inflict a telling blow on camp morale, perhaps deflate the fighting spirit of his adversaries, shake them up enough to give his little team an edge. There would be no immediate impact on firepower—that would have been too much to ask for—but the shock effect would still be worth it.

Three sentries had been posted on the ammo dump, and they were standing fast despite the general chaos in the camp. The nearest man saw McCarter coming and called out a warning to his friends.

The Briton came in firing from the hip. The guerrilla who had seen him first was also first to die, a ragged line of holes erupting from his waistline to his throat. The other two were breaking off in opposite directions, firing as they ran in search of cover.

McCarter nailed the gunner on his right, a sweeping burst that cut the man's legs from under him and dumped him facedown in the dirt. He lost his rifle, tried to drag it back despite his pain and shock, until another short burst found him and extinguished the remaining spark of life.

And that left one.

The Phoenix Force commando saw him drop into a trench where wooden crates were stacked in tidy rows. He hit the deck as bullets started searching for him, muzzle-flashes marking the location of his enemy, and palmed a frag grenade. He pulled the pin and made the pitch on instinct, knew that it was good almost before the lethal egg had left his hand. It wasn't how he planned to hit the dump, but it would have to do.

McCarter pressed his face into the dirt and waited for the earth to move.

AT FIRST Chuan Sukreepirom thought it was an earth-quake, Mother Nature stepping in to aggravate the problems he already faced. A moment later, when the giant, fiery mushroom hurtled skyward, his mistake was evident. A second shock wave rippled through the camp, and he was forced to squint against the rush of superheated air that swept around him like a draft from hell.

The ammunition stores had gone. How many soldiers with them?

Cursing to himself, Sukreepirom moved through the shambles of his base camp, shouting orders at his troops. They were disorganized, for all his training and instruction, discipline unraveling before his very eyes, and there was little that he could do about it.

He didn't have a notion who his adversaries were, nor how many were attacking. He didn't think they were official troops, or else they would have come in helicopters, raining death upon his soldiers from the sky.

But who, then, could they be?

There was no time for idle speculation. Half the men in camp were firing weapons, most of them without a clear-cut target, while the other half were more concerned with getting out alive. Sukreepirom's movement had been troubled by desertion from the start, a common drawback in the kind of "people's army" that relied on peasants cursed with short attention spans and limited conceptions of the sacrifice required to prosecute a revolution. He lost a few men every month and replaced them with new faces, but this night was the first time anyone had come against their jungle sanctuary, and it was appalling how his soldiers broke and fled.

Two soldiers passed him, running in the opposite direction, and he caught one of them by the arm and spun him, his open palm impacting on the young man's cheek.

"Where are you going?" the guerrilla leader demanded. "Would you shame yourself and me?"

The soldier blinked at him, as if emerging from a nightmare, startled to discover he was still alive and well. "They're everywhere!" he said. "The enemy!"

"Then you should have no trouble killing them," Sukreepirom replied.

"But I—"

"Will do as you are told." He wedged the muzzle of his side arm beneath the young man's chin. "If you are brave and do your job, you have a chance to live. If I suspect you are deserting me, I have no choice but to eliminate you, here and now."

The young man swallowed something bitter, grimacing, then gave a jerky nod.

"Very good. Now come with me and let the others see your courage. We must rally them and crush our enemies, before it is too late."

The soldier's grim expression left no doubt that he believed it was already too late for the camp, but he fell into step beside his leader as the man headed in the direction of the burning ammunition dump.

The enemy was "everywhere," but Sukreepirom had yet to see one of his adversaries in the flesh. Alive or dead, he meant to find one in the next few moments, try to find out something about the men who came to kill him in the night.

A secondary blast ripped through the ammo dump, spraying shrapnel over nearly one-quarter of the camp. His soldiers would have nothing but the ammunition carried on their belts and in their bandoliers, Sukreepirom realized. Enough, perhaps, to beat back this attack—or maybe not.

And if they did succeed, what then? The camp was lost, whatever happened. He would have to relocate with his survivors, start all over at collecting arms and supplies, convincing villagers to donate food and clothing, sons and husbands to the cause. The stinging memory of a defeat wouldn't be helpful when it came to scrounging for support. The people liked to back a winner, when they could— they had seen enough of hopeless causes in their dreary lives.

A victory, however, would be something else.

The prospect almost made him smile, but Sukreepirom had much to do if he was going to retrieve some measure of his dignity.

The first thing he needed to do was stay alive.

The second was to find his enemies and crush them underfoot like insects, wipe them out as an example to the government in Bangkok.

And to achieve those goals, he needed fighting men.

The guerrilla leader moved on through the killing ground, collecting soldiers as he went. The showdown was upon him, and he needed every man at his disposal if he hoped to see another sunrise.

KATZ WAS THIRTY PACES from the motor pool and closing when a burst of automatic weapons fire chewed up the ground in front of him and sent him sprawling to the deck. He hadn't seen the shooter, but he had a fair idea of the direction that near-miss had come from, and he faced that way, his AK-47 tracking, searching for a target.

The gunner rose from where he had been crouching seconds earlier, perhaps believing he had scored a hit. He was advancing, lining up another burst, when Katzenelenbogen shot him in the chest and pitched him over backward, dead before he hit the ground.

Katz scrambled to his feet and continued toward his destination, darting glances left and right as he proceeded to the motor pool.

The rebels had two flatbed trucks, three military-style jeeps and an old van they had converted to a rolling gunship, painted primer gray to merge with city traffic, windows tinted to prevent a passing cop or motorist from peering in. The extra fuel was stored in drums and jerricans, lined up behind the vehicles, and Katz made that his first stop, fastening a fist-size charge of plastique to the middle drum in line. When that one blew, the rest would follow, and there would be no way for the rebels to preserve their rolling stock.

Katz covered all his bets by dropping two more charges in a couple of the vehicles—one truck and the converted van—with timers counting down from thirty seconds. He was clearing out, when bullets started whispering around his ears, and he was forced to hit the deck a second time.

He watched for muzzle-flashes, spotted one and answered with a short burst from his own subgun, rolled to his left and came up running toward the camp latrine, some thirty feet away. It would be poor concealment, but infinitely better than none.

A bullet plucked at Katz's sleeve while he was running, and he made a headlong dive for the latrine. Plywood and corrugated steel had been employed in the construction, nothing that would stop a rifle bullet, but at least the sniper couldn't see him. It didn't stop the guy from firing, though, some of his bullets drilling cleanly through the thin walls.

Any second now...

The motor pool disintegrated with a roar that shook the compound, spewing jets of burning fuel in all directions, gas tanks going off like giant fireworks as the flames took hold and went in search of something else to burn. Katz took advantage of the instantaneous confusion to desert his cover, circling toward the point where he had seen those muzzle-flashes moments earlier.

The sniper was distracted, gaping at the light show, momentarily forgetting that he had a live one on the line. It came back to him in a rush, with Katzenelenbogen charging from the shadows, but his chance was gone, the rebel crying out in anger and frustration as he tried to bring around his gun.

Too late.

Katz stitched him with a burst of 7.62 mm slugs from twenty feet away, the rebel crumpling like a rag doll, triggering a final wasted spray of bullets in the air. Katz made sure it was done before he turned his back, eyes roving as he scanned the killing ground.

Not bad.

His heart was pounding, and he felt a little winded from the run, but he was hanging in there. Still on top. Not finished yet.

Not by a long shot.

A DRIFTING PALL OF SMOKE obscured the rebel camp as Bolan made his way past the perimeter, unguarded now. It reeked of gasoline, oil and burning human flesh, a combination that would tie the strongest stomach in knots. The smell brought grisly memories to life, recalling other battlefields, but Bolan focused on the here and now, aware that a distraction, even for a moment, would be all it took to get him killed.

He heard the enemy approaching, one voice barking orders while a dozen others answered, and knew that he had found his target. Chuan Sukreepirom was rallying the troops, too late to save his jungle stronghold, but the rebel chieftain's honor was still riding on the line. If he evacuated now, however wise it seemed, there would be questions later from the very men who followed him in flight. His leadership would be on shaky ground, and he would ultimately face a situation where his troops deserted him, or else a challenger came forward from the ranks.

If he had known that only three men were responsible for his embarrassment, Sukreepirom would doubtless have been more aggressive in his sweep across the compound. As it was, while he had to know his men had a numerical superiority, he couldn't tell if they were up against five guns or fifty, and his own ranks had been whittled down considerably in a hectic quarter-hour battle.

Bolan found his place behind the ruins of a four-man tent that had been trampled almost flat. He had a full clip in the automatic rifle, and he lined up his sights on the sound of boots and voices, which were drawing closer as a breeze picked up and started to unravel the protective smoke screen.

A dozen gunners came into focus, moving through the smoke like figures in a dream. Their leader was a man of average size, no special emblems or insignia to mark him, but his attitude, the orders that he snapped out to the others, said it all.

Chuan Sukreepirom was angry.

The AK-47 bucked and stuttered, tracking left to right along the line of dusty uniforms, the first three soldiers buckling, reeling, going down before their comrades understood the danger and began to scatter.

Sukreepirom stood fast, as Bolan had expected. He was carrying a submachine gun, the Chinese Type 64 with a ten-inch barrel that incorporated a silencer, the muzzle-heavy weapon spitting death in Bolan's general direction. His aim was a few yards off the mark, but he would correct that soon if he could sight on the Executioner's muzzle-flash.

A burst from Bolan's rifle found the guerrilla leader, rocking the man on his heels. He staggered, then dropped to one knee, fighting to maintain his balance even as his life ran out through ragged holes in his chest and abdomen. He snarled at Bolan, hanging on through sheer determination, but he couldn't keep his weapon steady long enough to make a killing shot. The submachine gun's muzzle became plugged with dirt as Sukreepirom slumped forward, and the weapon kept him from collapsing altogether, serving as a kind of brace, its butt wedged tight against his leaking chest.

The rest of the leader's assault force fell apart when he went down. A couple of gunners tried to return fire, but Bolan killed them in their tracks. The others scattered like a flock of chickens running from a hungry fox, some of them dropping rifles in their haste to get away. He didn't bother chasing them with bullets, recognizing that their nerve was broken.

They were done, and so was Bolan...for the moment.

Reaching for the two-way radio he carried on his belt, he raised it to his lips and spoke into the tiny microphone. "Fall back," he said. "We're out of here. Repeat, fall back."

McCarter's voice rasped from the radio. "Affirmative."

Katz took another moment, but he sounded fine. "I'm on my way."

Withdrawal from a hot zone was a tactic that required some practice, and Bolan knew the fine points from experience. The rebel camp's surviving troops were more concerned with finding cover now—each soldier looking out for number one—than with discovering and rooting out their faceless enemies. Whatever dreams they cherished of a new regime had all been washed away in blood.

And it was time to disengage.

The battle had been won, but Bolan's war in Thailand wasn't over yet. He had more enemies still waiting for him in Bangkok.

And Lao Fan was at the top of Bolan's hit parade.

4

Bangkok

Lao Fan had made his home outside of Chinatown deliberately. While *of* the people, it wasn't always so pleasant to be *with* the people, living every day with those whose tiny shops helped to support him through their tribute, lowly peasants who aspired to greatness but would never reach it, for the reason that they lacked the killer instinct necessary to succeed.

The house Fan had purchased for himself was located on Taksin Road, west of the Chao Phraya River and thus separated from the heart of Bangkok, as it was from Chinatown. Most days, weekends excepted, he would ride north in his limousine, make his way to Chinatown and let himself be seen transacting business, keeping up the image of a red pole who was both accessible and inescapable. Those who would beg a favor knew where they could find him; those who feared Fan were well aware that they could never find a place to hide.

He hadn't gone to Chinatown this day, remaining at his home to wait for Xiao Kong. The news from Khon Kaen had come as a surprise, and while Fan had little sympathy for the guerrillas, their support had been a project near and dear to Kong. Since Fan's hill chief, in his wisdom, had agreed to their alliance with the Dragon, that meant Fan was involved in left-wing politics himself. It didn't suit him, but he understood that compromise was part of life. The trick was making sure your would-be allies gave up more than you did, felt the pinch more keenly when it came.

Kong was drinking black coffee and smoking thin brown cigarettes, a ritual that didn't seem to calm his nerves. He twitched and quivered like a child about to meet the headmaster at school, expecting to be punished for some misbehavior in the classroom.

"You believe this raid is linked, somehow, to the attacks in Bangkok?" Fan asked.

"What other explanation could there be?"

"Perhaps the government . . ."

Kong dismissed the notion with a flutter of his bony hand. "Impossible," he said. "If the regime had scored a victory of these proportions, they would shout it from the rooftops. Instead, the army is 'investigating the disturbance.' They don't know what happened any more than we do."

"You had become attached to Chuan Sukreepirom, I realize." Fan's tone was condescending, with the barest touch of innuendo.

"Filthy rumors!" Kong spit back at him. "The man was useful for advancement of the People's Revolution, nothing more. Now I must start all over, make a new beginning, but I can do nothing until *you* identify and crush our enemies."

"I'm working on it," Fan stated.

"Without success."

"These things take time," the red pole answered stiffly, feeling angry color in his cheeks. "We don't all have a secret spy network on call for such emergencies."

Kong stubbed out one brown cigarette and lit another instantly. "My people have no information on the men responsible," he said. "Americans, they think, from the descriptions out of Europe, but that's all I know."

"Not very helpful, you'll agree." Fan couldn't resist an opportunity to twist the knife.

"Still, with your influence in Chinatown—"

"I've passed the word throughout Bangkok," Fan assured him. "If your round-eyes come within a mile—"

The big house shuddered, rocked to its foundation. The explosion echoed through its rooms and corridors, defeating Fan's first attempt to isolate the source. It seemed to come from everywhere at once.

Fan jumped to his feet, shouting for his men. Across the table, Kong seemed more relaxed than he had been at any time since his arrival. When he spoke, his voice was thick with irony.

"Was that a mile away, do you suppose?"

THE RUSSIAN RPG rocket launcher is simple to operate. A 39-inch metal tube with pistol grips and sights attached, it weighs fifteen pounds unloaded and can hurl its awkward-looking five-pound missiles with sufficient accuracy to disable tanks or bring an aircraft spinning back to earth. Effective range for moving targets is 330 yards, but you can add 220 more for stationary targets.

Like a house.

In fact, the Executioner was much closer when he loosed his first high-explosive round at Fan's mansion. Geography and strategy prevented him from laying back 550 yards to blast the house and grounds with rockets. He was counting on the RPG to get things rolling, but he also meant to get inside, if possible, and verify the kill. It wouldn't be enough for him to simply trash the house and fade away, while Fan brushed the dust off and went back to selling heroin around the world.

The Phoenix Force warriors were on station, waiting for the signal to advance. They got it when the first round from Bolan's RPG sheared off a yard of railing from the second-story balcony, crashed through a window and ex-

ploded somewhere in the house. The Executioner loaded
the second one immediately, sighting on the front porch,
where several Triad gunmen stood together, arguing about
what they should do.

He broke the deadlock for them, placing another high-
explosive round on target. Smoke and flame enveloped the
gunners in a heartbeat, shrapnel ripping into them like
knives. He cleared the porch, reloading swiftly as he advanced on the house at a dead run.

It had been twenty hours since the raid at Khon Kaen,
sufficient time for the return flight with their outlaw pilot
and additional reconnaissance in Bangkok, tapping Reid
Delaney for a lead on Xiao Kong. It was predictable that
Kong should run to see Lao Fan when he got word about
the rebel massacre in the north. It was unlikely that the men
would pass for friends, considering their varied back-
grounds and beliefs, but they were cast as grudging allies
for the moment, and Kong had no troops to protect him
once the rebels were annihilated. It was only logical, there-
fore, that he should look for sanctuary with the 14K.

But there was no safe haven to be found in Bangkok,
while the Executioner and company were on the prowl.

He was in blacksuit, carrying a Chinese-made AK-47,
with a Browning double-action automatic slung beneath his
arm. His web belt and the bandolier that crossed his chest
both carried extra magazines, along with frag grenades—
the Russian RGD-5 antipersonnel model so popular with
terrorists around the world.

The house was burning now, smoke drifting from the
shattered upstairs window. It would keep some of the soldiers busy, putting out the fire, and anything that managed to distract them was a plus for Bolan and his comrades
at the moment.

A cautious squad of Triad gunmen was emerging from
the house, stepping over twisted bodies on the porch, prepared to fire on anything that moved. Their first glimpse of

the Executioner was startling enough to make the pointman hesitate before he called a warning to the others,
bringing up his submachine gun to defend himself.

Too late.

The AK-47 stuttered, chopped him down and nailed the
gunner standing just behind him, making it a double play.
Three others broke for cover, two retreating toward the
open door, while their companion dropped into a fighting
crouch and started pumping bullets toward his adversary.

It didn't help him. The Kalashnikov erupted with another burst that sprawled him across the smoking body of
a comrade killed by Bolan's RPG. The two survivors huddled just beyond his line of sight, and the Executioner knew
that he would have to clear the doorway if he meant to
make his way inside the house.

He palmed a Russian frag grenade and yanked the pin,
running toward the porch. It wouldn't be an easy pitch if
he was under fire, but it could still be done.

The options were to give it up or die in the attempt, and
neither struck him as acceptable. He made the toss from
thirty feet, saw one of his opponents duck back as the hand
grenade bounced off the doorjamb, dropping almost at his
feet. A strangled cry of panic was obliterated by the smoky
thunderclap of the explosion.

Done.

The warrior charged the porch and cleared the threshold
in a headlong rush.

McCARTER WAS UP and moving after the first rocket detonated, coming in behind Fan's detached garage. He heard
the second RPG round strike the house, somewhere beyond his line of sight. He hoped there weren't too many
guns in residence tonight, but he would do his job regardless, take it all the way.

He had already cut the phone line to Fan's residence.
That wouldn't stop the red pole calling out for reinforce-

ments on a cordless telephone, but it should buy a few more
seconds, anyway, and that could make the crucial difference. Any troops Fan reached out for would be forced to
make the drive from Chinatown, half an hour away in
traffic.

And McCarter knew that half an hour could be a lifetime.

He was rounding the garage when the Mercedes-Benz
went up in smoke. Immediately to his right, a gunman
standing guard on the garage was staggered by the blast,
disoriented, weaving around so that he faced McCarter,
blinking startled eyes. The guy was packing, but he wore
the pistol underneath his jacket, well around in back. As
shaken as he was, and with McCarter's AK-47 aimed directly at his face, he did his best to reach the weapon.

No such luck.

A 3-round burst ripped into him and pitched him backward, halfway toward the flaming wreckage of the Benz.
There was no question of his rising, and McCarter had dismissed him by the time his body hit the pavement, moving
onward toward the house.

Fan's soldiers didn't know which way to turn, with three
explosions nearly circling the house, and now McCarter's
gunfire out in back. He had reduced the gap to sixty feet
when three young guns spilled through the nearest doorway, looking first toward the Mercedes, sighting in on
McCarter next as he rushed at them through the firelight,
blasting on the run.

He nailed the pointman with a disemboweling burst that
spun him on his heels. The survivors broke to right and left
instinctively, one brandishing a shotgun, while the other
held a stubby SMG.

In basic training, a soldier was taught to pick and choose
between targets in emergencies, take down the man who
posed the greatest threat by virtue of proximity, the type of
weapon he was packing or a dozen other factors. The odds

were fifty-fifty, in McCarter's situation, whether automatic fire or buckshot was more likely to reach out and bring him down. He knew that he had to stop both adversaries cold, before one of them got the range and finished him.

He held down the AK-47's trigger and swung the muzzle in a fiery arc, no careful marksmanship involved. It was the kind of situation where a heartbeat's hesitation meant disaster, and the only guide a soldier could depend on was his instinct for survival. Kill or be killed. Do or die.

He caught the young man with the shotgun first, a rising burst that lifted him completely off his feet and threw him into a clumsy backward somersault. There was still time enough for number three to make the kill, but he was frozen for an instant as he saw his second comrade die.

And that made all the difference in the world.

McCarter shot him in the face from twenty feet away, the gunner's head exploding like a melon packed with fireworks. Past the dead men, putting on more speed, he reached the back door of Fan's house.

He smelled wood smoke as he edged inside. The place was burning, which came as no surprise, but it would generate more pressure, reduce the time that he could spend inside. McCarter didn't want to think about the seconds ticking by, time slipping through his fingers, but it was impossible to quash the thoughts entirely. Every battle was conducted on a deadline, some more strenuous than others. Here, he faced his enemies, the prospect of police arriving any moment, and the house was burning down around his ears.

No sweat.

If he could find the people he was looking for—Lao Fan or Xiao Kong—it would be simple to complete the sweep and make his getaway. Of course, Fan's soldiers might have other plans, as would the first policemen on the scene.

McCarter kept his wits about him, checking out the kitchen as he passed. The hunter kept on going, searching for his prey.

IT WAS APPARENT, early on, that Xiao Kong would have to slip away from Lao Fan if he meant to save himself. The red pole was infuriated by the very fact that anyone would dare attack his home, committed to a stern defense, while logic told Kong that they should flee, leave men behind to do the dirty work and let police sort out the problem while they made their getaway.

Kong said as much and got a sneer from Lao Fan for his trouble, with a lecture on the Triad's code of "honor." Under other circumstances, Kong would have laughed at him, a pimp and dealer in narcotics ranting on about his sacred pride, but that wasn't the time or place. Fan was on the verge of an explosion, brandishing a pistol he had taken from his desk and barking orders at the gunmen who ran in and out to get directions from their leader. Pushed too far, he could as easily shoot Kong as any round-eye he discovered in the house.

Kong had a weapon of his own, the pistol tucked into his belt beneath his jacket, but he dared not use it on Fan unless there was no other way to save himself. The worst thing he could do was to give the red pole any reason to suspect that he, Xiao Kong, was somehow working with their common enemy.

But he would have to slip away, regardless. He couldn't wait here while Fan acted out some mock-heroic fantasy and doomed them both. Kong was no more anxious to be questioned by police than he was to be killed by some wild-eyed American adventurer. His usefulness in Bangkok was dependent on the veil of secrecy that he had drawn about himself, the fact that he had never been detained or grilled by state investigators, never publicly connected to the machinations of Beijing.

"Come with me."

It was an order, Fan talking to him as if Xiao Kong was one of his employees, a pathetic underling, instead of an equal partner in their joint enterprise. Kong stiffened, bit off the response that came to mind and simply nodded. Fan led the way out of the office-study, gunmen waiting for them in the corridor outside like a protective palace guard.

"That's smoke." Kong didn't mean to speak the thought aloud, but there it was. Fan stared at him, his features stuck somewhere between disinterest and contempt.

"The house is burning," one of Fan's soldiers said, then turned away with eyes averted when the red pole spun to glare at him.

"I have no use for cowards," Fan stated. "If any one of you desires to run away, go now. Disgrace yourself forever and be gone."

Kong turned without a word and started back along the corridor toward the kitchen and the property beyond. Fan had a garage there, perhaps a vehicle with keys in the ignition. Otherwise, it was a walk of three or four miles back to Chinatown. It should be no problem in the darkness, if he watched his step and didn't make himself too obvious before he found a place to hide.

"Xiao Kong!" The angry voice lashed out to sting him like a whip.

He hesitated, turned and found Fan staring at him, wide-eyed, like a madman. "*You* are leaving?" he demanded.

"I do not propose to stand inside a burning house," Kong said, "and wait for unknown enemies to shoot me down. That may be cowardice to you, Lao Fan. I call it common sense."

Fan's soldiers glanced at one another, muttering, but they all turned to stone before the red pole's angry glare. Fan turned back to Kong and couldn't help coughing from the smoke as he prepared to speak again.

"So, this is how a hero of the People's Revolution fights his battles. *Colonel* Kong, the mighty warrior! I've known women with more courage."

"May they serve you well," Kong replied, and turned his back again, ignoring Fan's ranting as he made his way along the corridor.

At first he was afraid the red pole would have his soldiers open fire, or chase Kong down and drag him back, but in another moment there was silence from the man, and his party didn't follow.

The first thing Kong saw, emerging from the house, were three dead bodies scattered on the grass—Fan's men, beyond a shadow of a doubt. Not far away, the sleek Mercedes-Benz Fan favored for his trips to Chinatown had been reduced to smoking rubble, possibly by a rocket of some kind.

Kong glanced around, saw no one to oppose him and struck off toward the detached garage.

Why walk, when he could ride?

IT WAS THE KIND of situation Katz had once taught younger, greener soldiers to avoid. He was pinned down, his cover marginal, with two guns pouring lead at him from different angles. Any time now they would find a third man to triangulate their fire, or one of those already dogging him would get the bright idea to circle wide around and snipe him from the rear.

There had been no apparent problem starting out. Katz waited for the signal, heard the first round from the RPG strike home and was moving by the time the second missile found its target. His selected course led past the swimming pool and the tennis court, then across a marble patio to reach the house through sliding doors of glass.

He almost made it, but a near-miss didn't count.

It fell apart when Katz was passing the swimming pool. One gunner started firing at him from the broad doors of the patio, while yet another cut loose from upstairs. They missed him with the first few rounds, but luck could only stretch so far, and he was running out of options in a hurry.

So he jumped into the pool.

It was a shock at first, cool water on a muggy night, but Katz was more concerned about exposure to the hostile guns. His own weapon was wet now, but the AK-47 and its Chinese knockoff had been built to function in the worst conditions. It would last a while, and maybe even fire a few rounds while submerged, but the less time he spent in chin-deep water, the better it would be for his supply of ammunition and grenades.

He palmed a frag grenade, pulled the pin and dropped it to sink beneath him. Bobbing up just long enough to get an angle on the tall glass doors, Katz caught a spray of concrete chips from bullets striking near his face. It was a decent try, but no cigar.

He had the range now, risked himself once more to make the pitch, with bullets from the upstairs window raising tiny water spouts a yard behind him. Katzenelenbogen waited for the blast and came up firing, clinging to the pool's lip with his metal claw while he unloaded on the guy upstairs.

It worked.

His bullets caught the shooter, who was leaning out to see what had become of his support below. Already perilously overbalanced, the man lost it when he started taking hits above the waist. He spilled headfirst out the window landing in a crumpled heap on deck.

Katz scrambled from the pool, half slipping back before he caught himself and sloshed onto the deck. He stood, dripping, shaking himself to unload some of the extra weight his clothing had absorbed. He was about to check his weapon, clear the chamber, when a crashing sound from the nearby garage distracted him.

The first blow didn't do it, but a second split the bulging wooden door, and Katz was staring when a bright red

Porsche shot through the ragged opening, tires smoking on the pavement as its driver tried to take control.

Katz saw the Porsche aimed at him like a guided missile, headlights threatening to blind him, but he raised the AK-47, squeezing off a long burst toward the windshield and the man behind those lights. Bullets struck glass, some glancing off the sports car's hood before they found their target. It was difficult to guarantee a killing hit in those conditions, but he didn't really need a head shot. Flying glass and bullets were enough to shake most drivers, all the more if they were handling an unfamiliar car.

The Phoenix Force leader emptied the magazine, the Porsche already swerving to avoid him as his clip ran dry. He yanked another from the soggy bandolier across his chest and prayed the ammunition wasn't compromised by its submersion in the pool. The buck and rattle of his weapon reassured him, slamming more rounds into the careering Porsche, this time along the driver's side.

His adversary lost it, threw both arms up to protect his bloodied face and drove into the deep end of the swimming pool. The Porsche heeled over and sank to the bottom. With the windshield blown away, there was no buoyancy to speak of that could keep the car afloat.

No miracles.

The guy was still alive in there, limbs thrashing, bubbles streaming upward from his nose and mouth. Half out the driver's window, he was wriggling like some kind of eel before the Porsche touched bottom, twelve or thirteen feet below the surface. He seemed to stick there, something caught around his legs perhaps, and he was straining frantically when Katz unleashed a short burst from above.

The bullets didn't make it, leaving foamy wakes behind, like miniature torpedoes in an old war movie, swiftly running out of steam.

After thirty seconds, give or take, the last reserve of air exploded from the driver's lungs in silver bubbles, and he went limp on his perch. He appeared to hang suspended in the water, limp and lifeless, face up toward the surface.

It was only then that Katzenelenbogen saw the likeness, matched it to the passport photograph Bolan had received from his elusive contact in the local CIA.

The drowned man hanging from the Porsche was Xiao Kong.

Katz offered up a silent prayer of gratitude to the gods of war and turned away from Kong, in search of other prey.

THE FACT THAT BOLAN nearly missed Lao Fan was pure coincidence, that gremlin spawned by Fate and Luck that frequently bedeviled soldiers on the battlefield. They passed each other, more or less, as smoke spread through the downstairs rooms of the red pole's house. Fan's party came into the parlor from the formal dining room, while Bolan passed along a nearby corridor that took him *from* the parlor, in the general direction of the kitchen, pantry and the live-in servants' quarters.

Indeed, he might have missed them altogether, let them slip away into the night if Fan's rampant paranoia hadn't chosen that same moment to assert itself.

The culprit was a twenty-year-old guard, afflicted with a trace of asthma, who was starting to have problems with the smoke. He had begun to wheeze and fight for breath, hang back and let the others forge ahead without him. Fan saw the gap in their small ranks. "Hurry up and get in line!"

"I—I can't!"

"Damned insubordination."

Fan drew and fired his pistol in one fluid motion. There was no mistake about his aim. The bullet struck his target squarely in the left eye socket, snapped his head back and deposited his lifeless body on the floor.

The shot was like a beacon to the Executioner. He doubled back, homed on the sound and reached the parlor as the last of Fan's team was disappearing through French doors into a lavish flower garden.

He rushed the door, fired through it, following up with a sturdy kick that left his knee and ankle throbbing. Bullets swarmed around him as he crossed the threshold, plunging earthward from a flight of stairs immediately to his right.

A pivot to the right put him beneath the metal staircase, where his enemies would have to fire between their own feet to attack him, if they found an open space and wanted to continue the engagement. They were evacuating, though, as fast as human speed could carry them away from Bolan and his comrades. Going up was a novel approach, when they had to realize the place was burning. It could only mean a pickup.

The roof was flat enough to take a helicopter, strong enough to bear the weight if they could load and take off fast enough. At least one man would never make it, Bolan's bullets ripping through his back and flank before he lost it, tumbling back downstairs to land at Bolan's feet.

A couple of the gunners heard the sounds and turned to face the intruder, ready for a human sacrifice if that would help the others get away.

They wanted martyrdom, and the Executioner was happy to oblige. His AK-47 stuttered half a magazine and nailed them where they stood, their leaking shoulders flattened to the door. When they began to slide, with an assist from Bolan, they left crimson smudges on the paneling.

The last door opened onto the roof, where a smallish chopper waited, rotors gaining speed toward takeoff. Fan had to have called it in by radio or cordless telephone, since there had been no chopper on the grounds while Bolan and company were making their reconnaissance.

The warrior cut loose on them with everything he had, used up the last rounds in his magazine to rake the chopper where it sat. The pilot gaped at him, as if the man in black had sprung full grown from his worst nightmare. Grappling with the stick, he got the aircraft off the ground.

Bolan slammed another magazine into the AK-47's hot receiver, sighted down the barrel as the whirlybird began to rise and bank in the direction of the nearby forest. Fan's face was pressed against the bubble glass behind the pilot, his expression stuck somewhere between a snarl and a shout of triumph.

The Executioner gave it everything he had, running dry as the first dark plume of smoke erupted from the chopper's engine and the aircraft began to circle back in the direction of the house. It didn't seem to be a plan so much as something that the pilot and his second-in-command couldn't prevent.

The helicopter was directly in front of the soldier now, coming closer by the heartbeat, with nothing to suggest that it would veer away before it cut him down. He took the only course of action open to him, stepping out into space and plummeting twenty feet to hit the ground.

Old memories of jump school saved him—tuck and roll to keep from breaking any vital bones. The impact jarred him, all the same, but it was nothing next to the holocaust above when Lao Fan's chopper slammed into the top floor of the house, flipped over on its back and blew up on the roof.

The house was lost to fire now, bright flames licking from the open windows, smearing charcoal smudges on the walls as they burned through. He hoped his comrades were outside, both of them free and clear, that questions would be answered for him at the rendezvous when they regrouped.

Right now, his first task was to get there on his own, alive and well.

The warrior struggled to his feet and put the burning house behind him, jogging off in the direction of the nearby trees.

5

Phnom Penh

Strictly speaking, the government of Cambodia is an infant, barely three years old. This, despite the fact that King Norodom Sihanouk has occupied the Cambodian throne, more or less continuously, since 1941. At one point, in the early 1970s, King Sihanouk retreated to Beijing, to "rule" from exile, and his nation suffered through two decades of a vicious civil war that finally expanded to include an occupying force from Vietnam. A new constitutional monarchy, complete with two-party elections, was ratified in September 1993, and King Sihanouk—now in his seventies—was back on top, albeit ruling through a younger prince.

The era of the "killing fields" is well behind Cambodia today, though scars have lingered that may never fully heal. Tourism hasn't caught up with the new reality, so far, but you can see white faces on the streets from time to time, around Phnom Penh, and visitors from other Asian lands have learned to make themselves at home. Chinese, while constituting barely five percent of the Cambodian population, have demonstrated their usual flair for commerce, establishing a solid enclave in the capital, with links to fellow countrymen abroad.

It isn't all smooth sailing in the "new" Cambodia, however. The Khmer Rouge rebels, once on top with aid from nearby Vietnam, are still at war with Sihanouk and his pro-Western government. The fighting, which has gone on almost nonstop for thirty years, still claims its share of lives each week in the outlying provinces.

And then there are the Triads.

Normally McCarter would have counted them as small potatoes in Cambodia, a pale reflection of the great crime syndicates in Bangkok, Taiwan and the Philippines. An alternate trade route for China white, perhaps, but nothing to demand a hellfire visit from the Executioner.

This day, however, knowing what he did about the 14K's alliance with Beijing, he took a greater interest in the Triad's probable collaboration with Khmer Rouge forces that were working overtime to turn the clock back and restore a Red dictatorship. Their efforts would be financed by the ever-growing tourist trade on one hand, and donations from the Chinese secret service on the other.

It was time to shake that cozy operation, hear it rattle, watch and see what might fall out. Cambodia was ripe for picking, and it felt like harvest time.

McCarter stopped outside a Chinese pharmacy, with dried ginseng hanging in the windows, jars of multicolored powders lined up on the shelves within. He wasn't interested in folksy remedies this morning, and the only powder that concerned him now was white. The shop had been described by "knowledgeable sources" as a drop for heroin, from which the uncut China white would be retrieved for shipment to the trading ports of Kampot and Kompong Som. It didn't qualify as major traffic, by comparison with daily traffic in the Patpong district of Bangkok, but it was steady and dependable, worth shutting down, if only for the nuisance value it would cause the 14K.

The Phoenix Force commando walked in off the street and found a wizened gnome behind the counter, waiting for him. At a guess, the man could have been sixty-five or eighty-five; it was impossible to tell.

"Speak English?" McCarter asked.

"Some," the old man replied.

"I'm looking for your special drugs," McCarter told him. "*Yào.* You understand?"

The old man made it halfway through a shrug before he saw the pistol in McCarter's hand, its muzzle heavy with a silencer. He nodded, turning toward the back room of his shop.

"This way."

The Briton followed him behind the counter, through a beaded curtain to the storeroom where he kept his stock. The old man opened up an ancient metal locker, stepping back to let McCarter see inside. The bricks of opium were wrapped in oilcloth, stamped with Chinese characters and a distinctive moon that would identify the source to a prospective buyer.

"Where's the heroin?" McCarter asked.

The old man shrugged again, pretending ignorance. It might be possible to squeeze him, but McCarter had no stomach for interrogating senior citizens, especially when he guessed the man was no more than a lowly go-between.

"Okay, we'll play it your way," McCarter said, palming an incendiary stick. "You're out of business, mate."

He primed the fire stick, placed it gently in the locker and propelled the old man toward the front door of the shop. A second fire stick went behind the counter, making sure the place would be a total loss. The old man didn't seem outraged, or even terribly surprised. McCarter reckoned he had seen it all before.

They were standing on the sidewalk when the Briton said, "If you can understand me, here's a message for your boss. Ma Yu, right? You tell him this is the beginning. We're just getting started. Got it?"

McCarter didn't wait to see the old man shrug again. He was already pacing off the sidewalk, moving toward the next spot on his hit list.

PHNOM PENH IS SITUATED on the Mekong River, long familiar to Mack Bolan from another time, another war. A portion of his life was spent along that river, stalking human predators, and he had earned his lethal nickname there, with nearly one hundred registered kills. A younger Bolan had been sent across the border several times, from what was then South Vietnam, to penetrate Vietcong sanctuaries and administer rough justice to the butchers of another "liberation army."

He smelled the river, closing in on Phnom Penh's Chinatown, and felt the memories come flooding back. He had been younger then, still wet behind the ears in many ways, unconscious of the fact that predators were everywhere, infesting every race and nationality. It took a while for him to learn that lesson, but he had it now, and once the knowledge put down roots, there was no turning back.

Most of the other whites whom he had seen around Phnom Penh that morning had been diplomatic types or U.S. military, back in the advisory capacity that had begun with Vietnam. They were no more loved by some Cambodians these days than their predecessors had been by by the South Vietnamese, but there was little risk of being fragged or gunned down in the capital itself.

So far.

The Executioner was launching a guerrilla conflict of his own, but he didn't intend to let it straggle on for months or years. If he didn't complete his business in a day—or two, at most—it had to mean that he had died in the attempt. There was no middle ground. He would expect no quarter from his enemies, and he would grant none in return.

Phnom Penh had no high-rise buildings in the Western style. The "giants" of the city stood around eight stories high, and most of those were new, constructed after tough street fighting in the capital destroyed whole sections and depopulated neighborhoods. The office Bolan sought was on the fourth floor of a modest building, near the heart of

Chinatown. It was supposed to be a legal office—and, in fact, the lease was held by an attorney named Yong Chee— but he was seldom seen in court, and Chee's sole client, based on information Bolan had received from Stony Man, was Ma Yu, the 14K's chief muscle in Cambodia.

It was as good a starting point as any, Bolan thought. Not as direct as striking at the red pole first, but it would send a message, one of several Yu would be receiving as the day wore on and Bolan, with his Phoenix allies, worked his way around Phnom Penh.

The young receptionist was female, twenty-something, curious enough to see a white man on the premises that she forgot to smile.

"Yong Chee?"

She hesitated, almost long enough to make him think he had the wrong address, then nodded, reaching for the intercom. A glimpse of Bolan's Uzi stopped her, frozen where she sat.

He tried again. *"Zài nar Yong Chee?"*

She swiveled in her chair and pointed toward a door behind her, to her left.

"Okay, get out." A waggle of the Uzi got his point across, and she was moving in a flash without a backward glance.

The second door was marked with Chinese characters, some variation on the theme of "Private," he supposed. It didn't stop him from reaching for the knob and entering the private sanctum of Yong Chee, attorney for the 14K.

The sight of Bolan's Uzi was too much for a man whose life was rhetoric and legal documents. He raised both hands, staring at the gun instead of Bolan's face.

"Do you speak English?"

"Yes." The word was whispered, barely audible from twenty feet away.

"Stand up."

The lawyer rose, an awkward movement, since he kept his hands above his head.

"And put your hands down!"

Chee did as he was told.

"I have a message for your boss," Bolan said, stopping as a flicker of the captive's eyes combined with a soft scuffling sound. Someone was at Bolan's back.

He turned and swung the Uzi like a club, across the face of a young gunner with a pistol in his hand. The youngster had been too anxious for a head shot, or perhaps he meant to coldcock Bolan, capture him alive. In either case, his plan evaporated as the Uzi crushed his nose and drove him back against the doorjamb. Simple reflex action made him squeeze the trigger, two quick shots, before the submachine gun stuttered, four rounds drilling through his chest at skin-touch range.

Chee lay slumped across his desk when Bolan swiveled back in that direction. Blood pooled underneath him, soaking through the papers on his desktop, draining from a chest wound where his would-be savior's bullet had gone home. The lawyer's one good lung was sucking air when Bolan reached him, lifted his head enough to see the stunned expression on his face and lowered it again.

So much for sending messages to Ma Yu through his attorney. There was still a message here, of course, but it was open to interpretation.

Never mind.

He would have other chances to communicate with his intended target in Phnom Penh. The fight was just beginning.

Macau

IT ALMOST SEEMED to Cheung Kuo that he should check for new gray hairs each time he passed a mirror. All his troubles of the past two weeks were bearing down on him, their weight enough to crush an ordinary man, but still the Dragon kept his head up, focused on the goal that had become his life.

First North America, then Europe, now his unknown enemies had carried their campaign to Asia, moving ever closer to his stronghold in Macau. It never crossed Cheung's mind that he would be a target—not yet, anyway. Instead, he saw the natural progression of a purge directed at the 14K, beginning in America and working toward the Triad's seat of power in Hong Kong.

It was too close for comfort, even so. Kuo trusted Edward Wong, up to a point, but if the hill chief of the 14K was cornered, saw a chance to save himself by selling out his grudging ally from Beijing, it would be only natural for Wong to grasp at straws.

The Dragon couldn't let that happen, would dispose of Wong before he let things go that far, but at the moment, he still hoped the situation could be salvaged. They had suffered grievous losses, it was true—the Triad more than Kuo himself, in terms of men and property—but it wasn't too late to turn the game around.

His own prestige had suffered in the past two weeks, and there were those in power, in Beijing, who said that he should be removed, even eliminated, as a means of limiting potential damage to their cause. Kuo still had strong support, no doubt about it, but another loss or two could change the minds of even those who trusted him the most. If it was demonstrated that he couldn't stop the enemy advance in Thailand or Burma, it would only strengthen those who had opposed his plan from the beginning.

Now he had the first bad tidings from Cambodia, and it was all that he could do to keep from screaming. Kuo's anger felt like acid, eating at his stomach, tasting bitter in his mouth.

He had already done the best he could, in terms of warning his Triad associates. They knew all what had hap-

pened to their brothers in the West, as well as Bangkok and
Rangoon. The death of warlord Tuan Khoo had shaken
Edward Wong so badly that he couldn't speak at first.
When he recovered from the shock, Wong had begun to
threaten Kuo, imparting blame for the misfortunes he had
suffered in a series of attacks that nearly ringed the globe.
Kuo had persuaded him, by force of personality, to calm
himself and think again, but there was only so much Wong
could take. His troops would be uneasy, his would-be successors waiting for an opportunity to push him from the
seat of power and take over.

Kuo knew that he was running out of time, but there was
little more that he could do. He had great influence in
Cambodia, with the Khmer Rouge rebels, and there was a
chance they could assist him in disposing of his enemies. A
chance, but that was all.

There were no guarantees.

Kuo poured a drink to calm himself. The liquor seared
his throat, then spread to light a fire inside him. In a moment he felt better, but knew it was a temporary feeling, no
real solution to his problem.

Only death would cure his headache, one way or another. He could find his enemies and kill them, or prepare
to die himself. There would be no room in the Party for an
officer who conjured such great schemes and then stood by
while they were torn apart by round-eyes. No apology
would satisfy his masters if Kuo failed.

It was imperative that the Khmer Rouge understand what
was at stake. Cheung Kuo's successor, if he was eliminated, might not be so generous with guns and money to a
group of peasant rebels in Cambodia. Indeed, they might
be cut off altogether, sacrificed in an attempt to shield
Beijing from fallout if his plan failed.

The time had come for Kuo's friends to pull their weight
and help him end the threat that menaced all of them. If
they couldn't do the job, he reckoned they deserved to die.

Above all else, he had to find a way to save himself. It was imperative. The People's Revolution couldn't do without him. He was becoming indispensable.

If the gauntlet had been thrown down in Cambodia, the Khmer Rouge would pick it up. They had been trained and paid to fight, now it was time for them to earn their keep.

And, failing that, they would be free to demonstrate their loyalty to the cause by laying down their lives.

Phnom Penh

KATZ CHECKED HIS WATCH and peered down from the rooftop, waiting for his target to appear. Across the street, his quarry's vehicle was idling at the curb, the driver chain-smoking and dropping butts beside the car. He had been waiting close to twenty minutes with the engine running, and it crossed the stern Israeli's mind that something had gone wrong.

Suppose the man he was waiting for had learned of other raids around Phnom Penh, directed at the 14K. Would he remain at home, locked up in his apartment? Would he dare avoid the battle, when his red pole needed him the most?

It was more likely, Katz decided, that the guy was on the telephone, arranging distribution of his troops around the city, trying to avert disaster while he had the chance, before things went too far. He couldn't know it was too late already—for himself, at least. The moment he emerged, he would belong to Katz.

It had been written in the stars.

A nervous-looking soldier cleared the entrance to the building, glanced both ways along the sidewalk, then across the street, before he signaled to his comrades waiting in the lobby. Two more gunners followed, with an older man close on their heels, a final soldier bringing up the rear.

Katz had the target in his sights at fifty yards, a forty-five-degree down angle, as his index finger tightened on the trigger. He absorbed the AK-47's recoil with his shoulder, holding steady, sweeping the tableau across the street with automatic fire.

The Chinese honcho staggered, reeling, going down as half a dozen bullets ripped into his chest and abdomen. The rear-guard soldier bought it next, Katz cutting off the path of least resistance, trapping the rest of the team where they stood. One of them ducked behind the car, but then the driver registered exactly what was happening and blundered out to help. Katz caught him with a short burst to the chest that punched him back inside the car and left him slumped behind the wheel.

The surviving gunners bolted toward the lobby doors, and while he could have let them go, Katz reckoned that one living witness to the slaughter was enough. He tracked them with the AK-47's sights and dropped them both before they reached sanctuary, bodies sprawled together on the pavement, crimson streamers racing toward the curb.

All right.

He broke down the rifle and stowed it in a worn athletic bag, retreated from his sniper's roost and hurried down the service stairs to reach the next street over. He stood out in the crowd, but no one tried to hinder his escape. If they were conscious of the shooting, it wasn't apparent from the faces passing by.

Katz felt the tightness in his chest begin to slacken, like a fist unclenching by degrees. The rental car was where he'd left it, and he let himself relax a bit more as he drove away.

So far, so good.

An inner voice reminded him that he wasn't finished yet. Katz scowled at his reflection in the rearview mirror.

Not finished, yet.

But he was getting closer all the time.

THE BOAT WAS EASY, but it left a trail. If Bolan blew it, had to ditch the craft somewhere when he was finished with it, there was no doubt that the owner would remember him and furnish the authorities with a description. Even so, it was an irresistible idea, too perfect to ignore.

He steered the speedboat north, along the west bank of the Mekong, passing docks and shabby live-aboards with ranks of warehouses behind them, looking for his target. Scouting from the landward side by car, he had discovered it was blue, a fresher coat of paint than many of its neighbors on the Phnom Penh waterfront.

The sky blue warehouse was a depot for the contraband that Ma Yu moved in and out of Phnom Penh on a daily basis, more or less unhindered by police and customs agents. Bribery, it seemed, worked just as well in a constitutional monarchy as it did in a democracy or a dictatorship. Low pay and slipshod discipline assured that there would always be someone in uniform who had a hand out, waiting for the chance to fatten his retirement fund or get a little something extra out of life right now.

He saw the warehouse up ahead and throttled back, continued far enough beyond his target that the Mekong's current would return him to the mark in seconds flat, once forward motion ceased.

The Executioner opened the heavy duffel bag that lay beside his chair, removed the Russian RPG and loaded it, the bulky HE round resembling a football that protruded from the launcher's muzzle. He was peering through the sights as he began to drift back toward the warehouse.

He had four rockets, and he meant to use them all before he gunned the engine, turned the little boat around and headed back to drop it off.

Round one was on its way before he came abreast of the warehouse, detonating on the loading dock as he was preparing number two. The shock wave came to meet him, rolling out across the water like a thunderhead, a whiff of smoke and carnage on the breeze.

His second shot went home within a yard or so of where the first had struck, making its way inside the warehouse and exploding there. Whatever Ma Yu was stocking at the moment, it was garbage now.

A handful of excited Chinese, stick figures at that distance, spilled from a side door of the warehouse, milling helplessly around, one of them pointing toward the boat as Bolan fired round three. It struck a corner of the warehouse near the eaves and peeled back a ten-foot section of the roof like the lid on a gigantic can of cat food.

His fourth round was a parting shot, the angle of attack already fading as he drifted farther south. Two trucks were parked outside the warehouse, near the loading dock, and Bolan turned the nearer of them into smoking wreckage with his final rocket. He dumped the launching tube into the Mekong and was at the throttle by the time scrap metal started raining among the men on the shore.

Not bad.

He hunched down in the driver's seat to minimize his height and chances were that another sailor passing by would file him in some mental data bank. There was a sixty-forty chance police would trace the boat, regardless, but the owner didn't know his name, and there were still enough white faces in Phnom Penh to drag out the search for a while.

The Executioner didn't need much time, another day at most, and he would be ready to move on.

The Cambodian police ranked well down on his list of worries at the moment. There were more important things to think about than winding up in jail. He had been snapping at a dragon's heels for two weeks now, and he couldn't avoid the thought that it had to wake and turn upon him soon.

The warrior wondered if he would be equal to that challenge when it came.

6

The day was young, but it had gone from bad to worse for Ma Yu. He didn't look forward to the afternoon and evening with anticipation, but rather with a sense of dread. His anger was a separate problem, one he could control, but fear was something Yu had left behind as a child—or thought he had.

But it was coming back to haunt him now.

Yu's life was focused on a passion for control. He had come up the hard way, through the Triad ranks, by working overtime to make himself the best, most ruthless gangster he could be. Yu had denied himself those pleasures that seduced his brothers into sloth and negligence. He saw their weak points and never failed to act accordingly. As red pole for the 14K in Cambodia, he was charged with supervising a vast territory, moving drugs from Laos and Thailand down the Mekong, and—within the past two years, at least—coordinating action with the local front man for Beijing, as he played footsie with Khmer Rouge soldiers in the countryside.

Yu hated Ung Pang, the man Beijing had sent to "help" him keep things on an even keel around Phnom Penh. It was against Yu's principles to trust a Communist, but his antipathy toward Pang was also personal. The man was like a grinning worm, ingratiating when you met him, later dropping snide remarks and implicit criticisms into every conversation, letting it be known that he—and, by extension, his almighty masters in Beijing—was somehow better, wiser, more experienced than lowly thugs who made their living from extortion and the drug trade. How a Communist could ever take the moral high ground was beyond Yu's understanding, but he kept his feelings to himself, made no complaints when Pang felt duty-bound to make believe he was in charge.

And now this business coming at them out of nowhere. Yu had sent a car and four soldiers for Pang, with instructions that the "diplomat" had no choice but to make himself available. Pang would be angry, and Yu hoped the man tried to make a scene. But Pang wouldn't be that foolish. Giving credit to the devil, Yu knew that it took finely honed survival skills to last, much less to prosper, in Beijing. Pang had connections who respected him and valued his opinion. He wasn't about to throw all that away over some petty quarrel.

The problem now, however, went beyond a simple clash of personalities. Phnom Penh had been under siege since breakfast time, a series of attacks directed at the 14K that was unprecedented in Yu's personal experience. He had no living enemies around Phnom Penh who would be brave or strong enough to risk his fury in this manner, which could only mean his adversaries had to be people from outside. And that, to Ma Yu, meant "Comrade" Ung Pang was probably responsible, at least in part, for what was happening.

Yu knew about the violence inflicted upon his brother Triads in the past two weeks or so, from San Francisco to Bangkok, but he hadn't believed the plague would touch him in Phnom Penh. His territory, while extensive and potentially a gold mine, was obscure, rarely considered when the DEA or Interpol sat down to list their top-ten "problem" countries. Everybody knew that Cambodia was a backward country, struggling to repair the damage done by thirty years of war and fratricide. It was the kind of country that you thought of briefly when a famine struck, or someone crashed a plane into the presidential palace with a bomb on board.

Which suited Ma Yu just fine.

He enjoyed working in the shadows, undisturbed by the harsh glare of publicity. Yu did his best work in the dark, but now he faced the prospect of a shooting war that would compel police to scrutinize his operation, and he didn't even know who his opponents were.

Not yet.

But he was trusting Ung Pang to tell him, very soon.

The man had to be good for something, after all. Why else should Yu permit him to survive?

A FRIENDLY CONTACT in Cambodia was even more important than it had been in their previous campaigns during the past two weeks. In a society where tourists were an oddity, white faces rarer still, Mack Bolan and his Phoenix Force allies would need all the help they could get from locals to spot their targets, keep the campaign well on track and running smoothly, with a minimum of risk beyond the norm.

The restaurant was three doors north, on Bolan's left. He walked past, glanced through the window and counted heads without appearing to take notice of the customers inside. He made it seven bodies, three of which were female and paired with men, talking while they ate. The odd man out was seated near the back and read an international edition of the *New York Times*.

That, barring any double cross, would make him Konerak Chamanand, described to Bolan by his Stony Man connection as a sometime contract agent for the Company who drew the line at any operations he deemed detrimental to his country and his king. He was supposed to be a hard-line anti-Communist who hated gangsters with the same abiding passion. That was fine, in Bolan's book, but he could do without a zealot hanging on his coattails, dragging some unwieldy personal agenda like an anchor that could get them all bogged down and slaughtered.

Bolan killed a moment window-shopping from the outside of a camera store, then doubled back toward the café. This time he went inside, brushed past the hostess with a smile and moved to join his contact at the table in the back.

"Mr. Belasko?" the Cambodian inquired in perfect English.

"In the flesh."

"I'm Konerak Chamanand. Please, sit down."

They shook hands after Bolan took his seat, a firm, dry grip from Chamanand to match his own. If the Cambodian was nervous, he concealed it well.

"How do you find Phnom Penh?"

"It's kept me busy so far," Bolan replied.

"Of course. Already the authorities are interested in your work . . . and others, too."

"I'm counting on it."

"You have colleagues in this effort?"

"More or less." He wouldn't name the others or expose them to this stranger before he knew that he could trust the man. "What I need now are leads, a way to make our efforts more productive."

"So, have you considered looking at the Khmer Rouge?"

"It crossed my mind," Bolan said.

"They are dealing with the 14K for weapons, I believe— or, I should say, they deal with Yu's new friend, the lizard from Beijing."

"That would be Ung Pang?"

"Correct. He funnels arms and ammunition to the Communists who would destroy our brand-new constitution. In return, they help guard Triad caravans of opium from Thailand, even some from Laos, I think. The Asian Communists are practical, Mr. Belasko. It is why the Chinese still stand fast, with Moscow and her satellites in chaos. Drugs mean nothing to the Party, by themselves. They still shoot dealers back in China, as I'm sure you know. But if their sale to Western nations undermines a future generation, leads to chaos in the streets...well, then, why not? All's fair in war, I think your people say."

"And paybacks are a bitch. We say that, too."

"You would be pleased to pay these devils back, I think," Chamanand said.

"It's why I'm here," the Executioner agreed.

"In that case, maybe I can help you."

"I was hoping you'd say that."

"But first, some wine. It helps me think, you understand?"

"Whatever's fair."

"And when our tongues are moistened," Chamanand went on, "we will devise the best way to annihilate our enemies."

The Executioner couldn't resist a smile as he replied, "Sounds good to me."

IT WAS THE HEIGHT of insolence for Ma Yu to summon Ung Pang this way, with gunmen waiting on the doorstep, showing him that he was bound to come, against his will if necessary. The move established a dangerous precedent, but Pang saw no point in debating it with the lower echelons when he could confront their master. Pang let his fury simmer on the ride from his apartment to the red pole's stylish home in a suburb of Phnom Penh, to the west.

The gunmen left him on Yu's doorstep, where a surly-looking houseman led him through familiar rooms and corridors to the westward-facing patio. Yu sat beneath a green umbrella near the swimming pool. His left hand swirled the ice cubes in a tall glass filled with tea or whiskey, Pang couldn't have said for sure.

"Sit down, please." Pang knew that Yu attempted to deceive him with a show of courtesy, after he was delivered, virtually at gunpoint, to the red pole's door. "Something to drink?"

"No, thank you."

"As you wish." Yu sipped at his own glass, then set it atop the wrought-iron table near his elbow. "We have business to discuss."

"Indeed?"

"You are aware of the attacks my men have suffered in the past few hours?"

So, that was it. "I heard a brief report," Pang told him, "on the radio."

"The details aren't important now," Yu said. "I think we both know this is linked to the unpleasantness in Bangkok and Rangoon."

Of course. An idiot could guess that much. Pang did his best to keep from sneering at the fat-faced gangster he was forced to call his comrade.

"Have you thought of a solution?" he inquired.

Yu responded with a frown and nodded. "I am shutting down all business in the city, as of now. Deprived of targets, even the best marksman cannot do us any harm."

"Your soldiers?"

"Will be scouring Phnom Penh for the round-eyes who are rash enough to twist the Dragon's tail. When I have dealt with them, we can return to normal operations."

"I should ask Macau," Pang said.

"Ask anyone you like," Yu replied, a sharp edge to his voice. "But don't forget who runs this town. We've come together in a common cause, but I am not some lackey for Beijing."

"I will be pleased to pass that message on to my superiors."

"Is that a threat?"

"By no means. I am simply one who follows orders. You know that as well as anyone."

The red pole studied Pang's face for a moment, seeming to relax somewhat. "Of course," he said at last. "We all have masters we must satisfy."

"It troubles me to think the actions of a stranger may destroy all that we've worked for since your hill chief and the Dragon made their great accord."

Yu was clearly troubled now. He raised a hand and waived it rapidly before his face, as if attempting to disperse a cloud of gnats.

"It was not my intention to suggest a breakdown in communication," Yu proclaimed. "Instead, I feel we should cooperate to crush our enemies, without delay. Perhaps if there was some way for the Dragon to assist us more directly..."

"I will be most happy to contact the Dragon on our mutual behalf," Pang said. "He looks with utmost favor on a spirit of cooperation."

"Excellent." The tension in Yu's face was somewhat lessened. "In the meantime, I have soldiers and investments to protect. It will be costly, closing down my operations for the time required to find these men, but it cannot be helped. Unfortunately, this will also interrupt the flow of weapons bound for the Khmer Rouge."

And retard their plan for toppling the Cambodian regime, Pang thought. He could have argued, but for once he thought the moon-faced thug was probably correct. It would be foolish to expose the latest shipment to a danger that wasn't yet neutralized. He wasn't fool enough to order that they rush ahead, regardless of the risk, and thereby jeopardize a shipment that would cost the Party several million dollars to replace.

A move like that wouldn't be good for his career, and while Ung Pang was a devoted soldier of the People's Revolution, he was also highly skilled at looking out for number one. A ranking Communist in China learned early on to watch his back and guard against the machinations of his so-called "comrades." Pang had made it to his present rank and station by observing those around him, recognizing when they wished him ill and striking before his adversaries had a chance to bring him down. Likewise, he had been quick to learn when it was better to do nothing, for a time, than to invite disaster by some ill-considered move.

"The rebels have been waiting for their victory since 1965," he told Yu. "I think it will not hurt them if they have to wait a few more days."

"We understand each other, then?" the red pole asked.

"Indeed we do." Pang smiled. "I'll have that glass of tea now, if it isn't too much trouble."

KATZ TURNED and asked McCarter, "Do you think we're going back into the jungle?"

"Couldn't say."

They sat across the street from the café where Bolan was supposed to meet his contact. It was pushing seven minutes since they watched him cross the threshold, telling Katz that he had found his man. With any luck at all, the trouble they had been detailed to guard against would never come to pass.

"I'm getting too damned old for this," Katz said, a bit surprised to hear the thought emerging audibly.

"Since when?" McCarter asked, glancing briefly at the gruff Israeli's face before he turned away and concentrated on the object of their primary intention.

"It's a feeling I have lately. Looking in the mirror, walking through the godforsaken jungle. Do you ever feel that way?"

McCarter flashed a cocky grin. "Not me," he said. "I'm indestructible."

"Well, that makes one of us."

The Briton turned back to face his friend. "You're bloody serious?"

Katz shifted in his seat, uncomfortable with the tropic heat and with the atmosphere of a confessional. "I haven't made my mind up yet," he said. "I may just need a holiday."

"You'll count me in on that, I trust," McCarter said, "when we get finished here."

Katz frowned. "The truth is, my thoughts were of a younger, more attractive traveling companion."

"So, you think I'm unattractive now?"

"Let's say you're not my type, and let it go at that."

"It's shocking, what we've come to," McCarter said, feigning outrage. "You think you know a person all these years, and then to have him plunge a dagger in your back . . . it breaks my heart, it does."

"I'll send you flowers. How would that be?"

"Candy would be better, if you don't mind."

"Not at all."

McCarter checked his watch. "You reckon he's all right in there?"

"Why not?"

"I'm not so keen on trusting total strangers in the present situation, if you follow me. For all we know, they could have grabbed him and run him out the back."

"We would have noticed," Katz suggested, "when the roof blew off the place."

"Unless they took him by surprise."

"You want to go inside and check?" Katz asked.

"He said wait here."

"That's right, he did."

"I'm bloody waiting, aren't I? No one said I had to like it, though."

He had a point. Katz didn't like it, either. It seemed everything was getting on his nerves the past few days—or weeks, now that he thought about it, making him consider the unthinkable: that maybe it was time to find another line of work.

Not yet, though. He was in the middle of a job, and he would see it through. With any luck at all, there might be time to think about his options later. And if not, well, then, Katz knew, the problem would have already resolved itself.

He reached beneath his loose shirt to adjust the automatic pistol in its shoulder rig and settled back to wait.

"YOU UNDERSTAND," Konerak Chamanand said, "that the Chinese are supplying arms and ammunition to the Khmer Rouge for their campaign against the king."

Bolan nodded. "I assumed as much."

"Thus far, most of the fighting is confined to several northern provinces. It's not as bad, yet, as the struggle twenty years ago."

"But getting worse."

"Indeed. The rebels have won certain victories, and they have strength enough to terrorize outlying villages. Where they find sympathy in short supply, the ranks are filled at gunpoint. A strategic execution every now and then works wonders on dissenters."

"I imagine so. The government must have a handle on their operations, though."

"The army chases them, fights skirmishes, interrogates suspected rebel sympathizers. It's an old, old story here. Of course, there have been certain accidents, as well, which afterward reflected badly on the government. The Communists make use of such events in propaganda, here and in Beijing."

"I understand the rebels are decentralized," Bolan said.

"In theory, that's correct. Their units in the provinces are more or less autonomous. They have a leader, though, for plotting broader strategy and doing business with the Red Chinese."

"Kriangsak Yodmani," Bolan stated.

"I'm not so sure you need me, after all," Chamanand answered.

"Sure I do, if you can tell me where to find him."

"Ah. Such information is most difficult to come by, as I'm sure you understand."

"How much?" Bolan asked.

Chamanand put on a wounded face. "Do not insult me, please. You think that I would haggle over money when my homeland's future is at stake?"

"I simply meant to cover your expenses."

"Well..."

"But I would need a pointer to Yodmani. No mistakes."

"All things are possible," Chamanand said. "You choose a dangerous direction for yourself."

"It's force of habit," Bolan told him.

"And if you should find the man you seek? What then?"

"We'll have a talk about political philosophy. We may have more in common than he thinks."

"How so?"

Bolan smiled. "In certain situations, I agree with Chairman Mao that power issues from the barrel of a gun."

"I can, perhaps, supply you with a map. As for the transportation..."

"I can pay. I've told you that."

"It's not for me, you understand. Bush pilots are a rare breed in my country—rarer still, the pilot with an airplane fit to fly. To risk his life, a man like that will have to know that it is worth his time."

"You fix the meet, I'll bring the cash."

"That is something I appreciate about Americans," Chamanand said. "Your ability to cut through, ah, how do you say it?"

"Bullshit?"

"Yes! Precisely!"

"So, we have a deal?" The envelope was khaki-colored, fat enough to hold a small fortune in currency.

"I will need two hours. Can you come back here at five o'clock?"

"Assuming it's still safe."

"I guarantee it with my life."

"That's right," the tall American replied. "You do."

7

Angkor

"The jungle," Katzenelenbogen groused. "I knew it."

Pausing for a moment on the trail, he swiped an arm across his forehead to remove the perspiration beaded there. The narrow strap on his Kalashnikov was chafing at his shoulder, and he shifted it for some relief.

"You're psychic," McCarter said, passing by him on the trail. "What can I say?"

Two hundred miles northwest of Phnom Penh, another fifty would place them on the Thai border, but they weren't going that far. Their destination was Angkor, an ancient city now in ruins, which Bolan's contact had named as a landmark in their search for the Khmer Rouge forces led by Kriangsak Yodmani.

They wouldn't find their prey in Angkor, that would be too easy, but a short jog southward ought to place them within striking range—unless, of course, the whole thing was a wild-goose chase.

Bolan appeared to trust the man who had directed them to this location in the jungle, even though the guy declined to tag along and play the role of guide. They wouldn't need him, if his information was correct, but Katz wished he was close enough to touch if anything went wrong.

He slogged along the trail behind McCarter, bringing up the rear, as dusk left shadows pooled among the trees.

There was no sign of any trickery or ambush yet, but it could still be waiting for them up ahead, or creeping up behind them in the forest. Anything was possible from a contact who might have been working both sides of the street.

They spent another fifteen minutes on the trail before the signal came from Bolan, on the point. They halted, stood in total silence, then started edging forward once again, more careful than before about their footing, watching both for booby traps and anything that would produce unwanted noise.

From somewhere up in front of them, Katz heard the sound of voices, with the odd clank of equipment now and then. No generator noises, but he smelled wood smoke and something cooking on the fire.

They reached the tree line moments later, Bolan easily directing them to left and right. Reconnaissance was the priority, collecting information on the camp and sharing it before they made their move.

Katz knew the game. He made no sound as he began to circle the perimeter to check out the tents that seemed to be the only shelter in the camp. From what he saw, it was apparent that Yodmani's troops had started with a jungle clearing some one hundred feet across, strung camou netting to conceal themselves from airborne searches, then proceeded to expand the clearing fifty feet on every side, until they roughly doubled its diameter. A fire pit had been excavated near the center of the clearing, and a giant cast-iron pot was mounted there, slung from a spit between forked stakes, flames lapping at its underside.

Katz started counting heads, aware that he wasn't expected to present a final tally. They would all compare their observations and try for a consensus. It wouldn't be perfectly precise, nor did it have to be. A few guns either way would make no difference to the ultimate result.

He crept on through the twilight gloom, deep shadows covering his passage.

IT HAD BEEN relatively simple, staking out the camp. Three men couldn't surround a camp, but Bolan had placed his Phoenix Force comrades in position to triangulate their fire with his at the beginning of the strike, and when they moved from that point onward, it was each man for himself, specific targets preselected, quarters of the camp assigned.

There was no guarantee it wouldn't fall apart. Once they began to move, their enemies reacting, it was anybody's game. The chaos factor couldn't be eliminated, but a savvy warrior knew enough to be prepared for any possible contingency.

Bolan checked his watch. Another thirty seconds remained before Katz and McCarter would expect his signal. He braced the loaded RPG across his shoulder, peering through the sights at his selected target, near the center of the camp. The photos he had seen of Kriangsak Yodmani had been fuzzy long-shots, five years out of date, but Bolan thought he recognized his man downrange, one of perhaps a dozen clustered near the cooking fire. If he was wrong, a rocket dropped into the middle of that crowd was still the best way he could think of to begin the battle, shake his adversaries with the first punch and press in from there until they swept the field.

He counted down the seconds in his head, knew when the time was right because he heard it click, as if someone had thrown a switch. His finger tightened on the trigger of his RPG, a searing tongue of flame lashed out behind him and the chubby five-pound missile sped off toward its target.

The explosion tossed a couple of Yodmani's soldiers skyward, tumbling like a pair of circus acrobats, while others sprawled or staggered backward from the epicenter of the blast. Some of them wouldn't rise again, while oth-

ers scrambled to their feet almost immediately, streaming
blood from shrapnel wounds and wiping dust out of their
eyes.

He had a second rocket loaded by the time the echoes of
the first blast started batting back and forth among the trees
behind him. Bolan searched his field of fire for Yodmani,
but he came up empty in the swirl of dust and running figures. Katzenelenbogen and McCarter cut loose with their
Kalashnikovs from the northwest and southeast quad-
rants, hosing the Khmer Rouge soldiers as they scattered for
their lives.

He aimed the second missile at another clutch of rebels,
pointing at the scene of chaos caused by the first explosive
round. They hadn't pegged the source yet, but the second
shot would mark him.

He let the five-pound rocket fly and dropped the
launching tube before the missile covered half the distance
to the target, scooping up his Chinese AK-47 on the run.
Downrange, a number of Yodmani's soldiers were already
pointing toward the spot where Bolan's second muzzle-
flash had given them a mark to aim at, squeezing off long
bursts of automatic fire that demonstrated more enthusi-
asm than skill.

Bolan broke to his left, running hunched over through
the trees and dangling creepers, hearing bullets rake the
foliage where he had been crouching seconds earlier. The
RPG was good for more than just delivering a knockout
punch; it also helped distract his enemies while he was on
the move.

His Phoenix Force allies would be moving, too, by now.
It was a fool's game to remain in place and duel with over-
whelming numbers, when the other side had spotted your
position and had time to organize a pincers movement,
flank your outpost and cut you off. Instead, the thing to do
was hit them hard and fast, do all the damage possible in
seconds flat, then close in to finish it at closer range.

He had already closed the gap by half, some ten or fifteen yards before he found himself inside the camp itself, and those of his opponents who had marked the backflash from his RPG were still unloading on the wrong location.

He fell upon them like the wrath of God, his AK-47 stuttering a song of death, its bullets slapping flesh and dropping bodies in his path before the rebels knew he had deceived them. Three of them were down, then four, five, others turning in their tracks to face him. All too late.

The Executioner had found them now, and there was no place in the world for them to hide.

KRIANGSAK YODMANI cursed bitterly and caught a soldier running past him, spun the man and slapped him full across the face. The private blinked and stared at him, as if emerging from a trance, but he made no attempt to break free of Yodmani's grasp.

"Control yourself!" the Khmer Rouge leader snapped at his disoriented underling. "Remember who you are!"

That was the problem—part of it, at least. Most of his men were peasants, volunteers or forcible draftees into a movement many of them didn't fully understand, in terms of revolutionary doctrine or the strategy of a people's war against the running dogs of Western Capitalism. Yodmani had been asking for Chinese advisers to accompany the guns Beijing provided, but they had been slow in coming. At the moment, Mao's disciples were more interested in trade agreements with America than spreading revolution in their own backyard, but the Khmer Rouge would fight on, regardless. They had managed to employ a few Vietnamese instructors, veterans of the long war with America, but they had been dispersed throughout the countryside, and none were in the camp at present.

Shouting orders as he went, Yodmani moved across the compound, reaching out to grab a frightened soldier here, directing others to a more secure position there, allowing them to see that he wasn't intimidated by their enemies, the threat of death. A leader had to lead; there was no substitute for strong, courageous guidance in the midst of death.

And his recruits were dying—there was no doubt on that score. The first explosion had come close to canceling Yodmani's ticket. The concussion knocked him sprawling, soiled his uniform with dirt and left a shallow gash along his hairline that sent crimson streamers trickling down his face. The pain was nothing, but he seethed at the indignity of being taken by surprise, knocked down before his troops and forced to scrabble on all fours like a demented beggar.

Some philosophers called pride a weakness, but Yodmani viewed it as essential in a fighting man. Why else would men fight on against imposing odds, if not to prove themselves—to friends and loved ones, in their own eyes, even to the scribes of history? If not for pride, the People's Revolution would be left to feeble-minded zealots or the sort who quested after martyrdom, preferring death to life.

Yodmani grabbed another soldier, and another, as he made his way across the camp. He wasn't frightened by the gunfire rattling all around him, knew that even if it meant his death, he had a job to do. He was a soldier, first and foremost. When it came his time to die, he wouldn't flinch or shirk his duty. They would find him at his post, still fighting, even as he gave his life up for the cause.

In moments, he had gathered fifteen soldiers, and the men who joined him rallied others to the fight. No longer were they rabble, but a fighting force once more. Still peasants, granted, but their arms and courage made them something more. Such men would give him everything they had—and at the moment, he would ask no less.

MCCARTER STARTED firing when the first grenade from Bolan's RPG exploded in the camp. He used up one full magazine before he scrambled to his feet, reloading on the move, and made his way through darkness lit by muzzle-flashes, closing with the enemy.

Before full darkness settled on the camp, he had confirmed that most of its inhabitants were young men. So it always was with revolutionaries who believed that they could change the world, young men with so much life ahead of them, until they made a foolish move and threw it all away.

Old soldiers were a different breed. They understood the give and take of life, of war, and were determined that death wouldn't take them any sooner than it had to. A professional would stop at nothing.

His opponents were disorganized, chaotic. Some of them were firing off into the jungle when McCarter fell upon their flank and cut them down. He moved past their crumpled bodies, found more targets waiting for him, seeming almost eager to give up their lives. Close quarters hampered the defense, some of the rebels firing on one another in the darkness and confusion. Friendly fire did some of his work for him, as McCarter swept on through the camp.

A hand grenade exploded somewhere to his left. The Briton glanced in that direction, thinking that he might glimpse Katz or Bolan, but neither man was visible in the frantic, swirling action. He wasn't afraid of firing on them accidentally—their camou uniforms and stature would prevent that kind of error, even in the dark—but they were out there, somewhere, and he had to watch his step, make sure his bullets went exactly where he meant for them to go.

A Khmer Rouge guerrilla stepped into his path, blinked at McCarter in surprise and tried to raise his weapon. He was almost quick enough to pull it off, before the Phoenix Force commando slammed down the muzzle and struck him with the butt of his Kalashnikov, a blow that carried force enough to crush the gunner's cheek and dislocate his jaw. The young man staggered, hanging on to conscious-

ness by sheer determination, dropping only when Mc-
Carter shot him in the chest at skin-touch range.

There were no buildings in the camp; it was a tent city
beneath a screen of camou netting strewn with leaves and
laced with branches cut from the surrounding trees. The
"motor pool" consisted of a flatbed truck, three motor-
cycles and an aging station wagon painted primer gray.
McCarter made his way in the direction of the vehicles,
avoiding certain rebels, dropping others when he couldn't
make his way around them unobserved. His mission didn't
call for indiscriminate assault on anything that moved. Instead, he was supposed to strike specific targets, raise as
much hell as he could without allowing anyone to tag him
in return and get the hell out of the killing zone.

A battle plan demanded flexibility, as when the two
young rebels saw McCarter moving toward the vehicles and
opened up on him from fifty feet away. Excitement and the
darkness saved him, offered him a fleeting second chance.
McCarter hit the deck in a flying shoulder roll and came up
firing from the hip with his Kalashnikov.

The nearer of his adversaries took a 3-round burst dead
center in his chest and toppled over backward with his finger frozen on the trigger of his submachine gun, bullets
streaming skyward as he fell. The other tried to dodge, but
he was focused on McCarter, and his feet got tangled up
with each other, tripping him. He fell across the Briton's
line of fire, the bullets ripping into him and spinning him
before he hit the turf.

McCarter rose and again started toward the line of waiting vehicles again, still focused on his mission. He had
plastique charges in the satchel slung across his shoulder,
more than he would need to leave the Khmer Rouge troops
on foot.

All things considered, it should be a relatively simple job.

THE KHMER ROUGE motor pool went up like a volcano, spreading shock waves through the camp. When the concussion hit Mack Bolan, he was sighting down the barrel of his AK-47 at a group of rebels forty feet away. They all went down together, Bolan and his enemies, as if a giant fist had swatted them aside. The Executioner was first back on his feet, and by the time the others rallied, he was raking them with automatic fire from his Kalashnikov.

The first two collapsed to the ground as the bullets ripped their flesh. Three others tried to break and run, one pausing long enough to fire a burst in Bolan's general direction as he turned to flee, but they had all run out of time. The AK-47 hammered at them, the Executioner close enough so that he had only to point the weapon, and they went down in awkward attitudes of death.

How many rebels left alive inside the camp? With the explosions, drifting smoke and various deserters heading for the jungle, it was difficult to say. A body on the ground was no firm guarantee of death. A soldier could be shamming, dazed or wounded, maybe waiting for the opportunity to put a round in Bolan's back as he passed by, but it would be impossible to check them all. He had to forge ahead, keep searching for the leader who had managed to survive his opening grenade attack.

And he found him moments later, Yodmani striding through the middle of the camp with better than a dozen soldiers following or flanking him. A rebel on the left flank spotted Bolan, aimed a finger at him, calling out a warning to his fellows. Half a dozen guns cut loose at once, and the warrior threw himself behind a nearby tent to prevent their zeroing the range. It wasn't much in terms of cover, with bullets shredding canvas as if it were tissue paper, chewing up the sod around him, whistling over Bolan's head.

He had to scatter them, and quickly, or he would be out of time and chances. Bolan palmed and primed a frag grenade, released it in a wild overhand pitch. From the screams that mingled with the blast, he knew his aim was adequate.

The Executioner burst from cover on the same side of the tent where he had last been seen, a ruse to fox the rebels who had seen him take his dive, if any of them were still looking for a fight. From all appearances, the frag grenade had taken half a dozen of them down, the others looking somewhat dazed but still alert enough to kill him if they got the chance.

He swept them with another long burst from the automatic rifle, bodies tumbling backward, reeling as the bullets found them and nailed them to the bloody earth. The Executioner caught a quick glimpse of Yodmani breaking for the sidelines, and he was after him, still firing at the gaggle of survivors. When his magazine was empty, Bolan ditched it, found another one by feel and reloaded on the run.

Yodmani had a slim head start, but he was going nowhere. Glancing backward frequently, he saw death coming for him, tried to turn and face his adversary, sprawling on his backside as he stumbled on the corpse of a subordinate. The rebel leader dropped his submachine gun, made a grab to fetch it back, but he was out of time. A burst of 7.62 mm manglers reached out for him from a range of twenty feet and flipped him over on his back, unmoving as his life ran out through holes in his chest.

The smoke was thick in Bolan's nostrils now, a reek of gasoline and motor oil, scorched canvas and roasting human flesh. It was remarkable, he thought, the way the smell of mortal combat never really changed, no matter where it was encountered on the globe.

He keyed the two-way radio clipped to his battle harness as he moved toward the perimeter. "Fall back!" he told his comrades, hoping they were both alive to hear him. "Disengage! Regroup!"

"Affirmative!" McCarter said, sounding glad to hear the order.

"Roger that!" Katz radioed.

So they were still intact, the three of them—but far from done with their campaign against the 14K and its supporters from Beijing. They still had debts to settle in Phnom Penh, prior to running down the next link in the chain.

Two weeks, and they were getting there, no doubt about it, but they still had far to go. He didn't even know their ranking adversary's name or where he could be found. Somewhere in the vicinity of Hong Kong or Macau, no doubt, but there were still more obstacles to circumvent before they got that far.

8

Phnom Penh

"It is unfortunate," Ma Yu said, "that nothing could be done."

His tone conveyed the message that he didn't find the rout of the Khmer Rouge troops unfortunate at all, but Ung Pang didn't rise to the bait. From where he sat, Yu recognized that his reluctant "comrade" had been shaken by the news from Angkor, the destruction of a force that had provided focus for his mental energy and cost Beijing so much in terms of money and matériel.

It would mean starting over...if Pang got the chance. His masters weren't known for understanding or forgiveness, even when the circumstances were beyond a subordinate's control. They loved to make examples of their fellow countrymen, as if one loss wasn't enough, without another heaped on top of it for emphasis.

In that respect, he knew, they had a great deal more in common with the Triads than most ranking Communists would ever willingly admit. Great minds, with but a single thought?

"You think it was the round-eyes?" he asked Pang.

"Who else? The army would be shouting its achievement from the rooftops otherwise."

"Perhaps they will be satisfied," Yu said, "and leave us now, in peace."

"Do you believe that?"

Yu considered his reply. Twelve hours had passed since they received the news from Angkor shortly after noon, and the battle had presumably been fought sometime last night. A full day, then, with no hint of renewed hostilities around Phnom Penh. It was enough to make him hope.

He was about to speak, some noncommittal pap, when three things happened almost simultaneously. In the yard outside, one of his soldiers shouted words that Yu couldn't make out. An automatic weapon cut loose, drowning out his voice, with others swiftly joining in the chorus, and a loud explosion rocked the house.

Pang bolted to his feet, while Yu was busy rummaging inside the top drawer of his desk, searching for the semiautomatic pistol he kept hidden there. The gun had always seemed superfluous before, with all his bodyguards around, but if the enemy was knocking on his door with rockets, Yu could do worse than to arm himself.

Or should he try to slip away?

Ferocious reputation notwithstanding, Yu had no great urge to join his brother red poles who had died during the past two weeks. He wasn't tired of living yet, and it wasn't his choice to exit life in a humiliating fashion—if he had a choice.

And that, of course, would be the problem.

If his nameless enemies had made it this far, battling halfway around the world and killing many in their grim war of attrition, was there anything Ma Yu could do to stop them? Were his soldiers any better than the troops in Bangkok, or the Khmer Rouge rebels who had fared so poorly in the jungle to the north?

Yu found the pistol, flicked off its safety and made sure it had a live round in the firing chamber. On his feet, he moved around the desk, his voice raised to call his bodyguards before he reached the door.

A second blast ripped through the house, but Yu suppressed a mounting sense of panic. Pang was close behind him, tugging at his jacket.

"What are you doing?"

"Getting out," Yu told him, barely glancing back. "Feel free to stay and meet our enemy if you are so inclined."

IT WAS MCCARTER'S TURN to use the RPG, and Bolan waited for the first grenade to find its target, detonating with a smoky thunderclap, before he left his cover at the tree line, rushing toward the house. Two smaller cottages out back were obviously quarters for the servants, with no activity apparent as he passed them by. He realized that news from Angkor had to have reached the capital by this time, which could only mean that Ma Yu and company knew what had happened to Yodmani's private army. It would stand to reason that the guards in residence would be on duty, in or near the house, instead of lounging in their quarters after dark.

He saw three of them, just coming into view beyond the swimming pool. They hadn't spotted Bolan yet, but they were on alert, two packing automatic weapons, while the third man had a shotgun. In the first rush of excitement, they forgot to spread themselves out to make it harder for an enemy to cut them down, and Bolan took advantage of the lapse. His AK-47 swept them with a burst from left to right and back again. The gunners reeled, stumbling into one another, going down.

He didn't stop to see if they were all dead where they lay, as it meant wasting precious time. He kept on moving toward the house, was fifty yards away and closing when a sniper with an automatic opened up on Bolan from a second-story window. Bullets started chewing up the sod in front of the warrior, veering to his left a bit as his assailant lost control, but he couldn't expect the same mistake a second time.

He fired a burst back toward the window, running serpentine to throw the sniper's aim off, hoping for a lucky hit. It was improbable at that range, firing on the run, but you could never tell. His bullets scarred the siding of the house, tore great chunks from the windowframe and shattered glass above the gunner's head, but Bolan couldn't tell if he was scoring on the man himself. If so, the wounds were minor, and they didn't stop his adversary from unloading with his submachine gun, spraying bullets into the yard.

It finally came down to speed, with Bolan flattening himself against the wall directly underneath the sniper's window. Now if his assailant sought to tag him he would have to lean well out across the windowsill and fire straight down, an awkward attitude that also left him physically exposed to gunfire from the ground. A sudden silence from the window told the Executioner his enemy had seen the problem and was doubtless moving to correct it, racing down the nearest flight of stairs to meet him, if and when he made his way inside the house.

To pull that off, though, Bolan had to find an entrance he could manage without getting slaughtered in the process. Working to his left along the wall, he checked one window, found it locked and was about to smash the glass when he saw someone moving inside the house.

Bolan couldn't tell whether he'd been spotted, but climbing through a window in the face of hostile guns was tantamount to suicide. He ducked below the windowsill and kept going, was about to reach a second when its sash flew up and one of Yu's commandos stuck his head outside.

The gunner from upstairs?

There was no way for him to tell, no time to think about it. Bolan's adversary saw him at once and reached back for a weapon. It was now or never.

Bolan rushed him, clubbed the startled man with his Kalashnikov, and grabbed him by his throat. He exerted force enough to drag him through the window, sprawling on the ground at Bolan's feet. A second buttstroke with the rifle crushed his larynx, left him dying where he lay, and Bolan seized the opportunity to peer cautiously through the window.

No bullets flew to meet him, no one shouted an alarm, and seconds later he was scrambling through the open window, landing in a crouch against the inside wall of what appeared to be a deserted recreation room.

Ma Yu and Ung Pang were somewhere in the house, and Bolan meant to find them both. He moved out, following the sounds of gunfire and excited voices speaking in Cantonese. Somewhere ahead of him, his enemies were waiting.

MCCARTER FIRED his first round from the RPG on schedule, watching as the rocket rode a tail of fire and struck the northeast corner of Yu's house, erupting smoke and fire on impact. He was smiling as he loaded up a second round, imagined Katz and Bolan on the move, advancing toward the house, while he distracted Yu's commandos with a pyrotechnic show.

"And for my next trick..."

The Briton lined up his second shot to put the rocket through a ground-floor window to the right of Yu's front door. The shot was perfect. McCarter watched as a fireball belched out through the window, bright flames licking at the woodwork of the house.

But he was running out of time.

A gunner standing in the yard pointed at him, shouting to his comrades. He had to have seen the RPG's dramatic backflash, comparable to a bazooka's. There was no way to conceal it in the darkness, and McCarter knew that he would have to move swiftly before they could surround him.

He took the launcher with him, tucked beneath one arm, two five-pound rockets clanking in the satchel slung across his shoulder. The AK-47 slung across his back was extra weight, too awkward for one-handed firing in the present circumstances, so McCarter drew his Browning automatic pistol from the holster on his hip. He kept moving to his left as first two gunmen, then a third and forth, ran toward him from the general direction of the house.

The darkness gave McCarter something of an edge, plus he was covered by the trees to some extent, a shadow flitting in and out among more shadows as he ran. The Chinese were firing now, but in the absence of another backflash from his RPG, they had no solid target. As it was, three of them carried submachine guns—which meant they were firing pistol ammunition with no greater range or stopping power than McCarter's Browning—while the fourth was armed with what appeared to be a U.S. Army-surplus M-1 carbine.

When McCarter made his stand, he put a bulky tree between himself and his advancing enemies, surveyed the angles briefly and prepared himself by balancing his pistol in a firm two-handed grip. The range was forty feet and closing, with his targets spread out in a skirmish line some thirty feet across, from end to end. His first shot would betray him, so he had to make it count.

He took the shooter with the carbine first, because his weapon's greater range and 30-round banana clip gave him more firepower, and also for the reason that dumb luck had placed him on McCarter's left, at one end of the skirmish line. He wouldn't have to jump around, this way, but could proceed from left to right until his adversaries went to ground or scattered to protect themselves.

The range had closed to thirty feet when he squeezed off a double-tap that put two bullets in the rifleman and slammed him on his back, heels drumming on the grass until the message reached his brain and he lay still.

The second man in line reacted to the shots and muzzle-flashes with a speed that almost spoiled McCarter's aim.

The gunner veered a long step to his right and fired a burst that came in high, the bullets gouging wood and shredding leaves a yard or so above the Briton's head. In answer, two more pistol shots rang out, 9 mm parabellum rounds exploding through the gunner's cheek and chest to spin him like a top before he fell.

The other two were trying desperately to save themselves. One pitched forward on his face to minimize exposure while he tried to find a target, while the other spun and took off running toward the house. McCarter took the runner first—a single round between the shoulder blades that propelled him through the air for several paces, finally dumping him in an untidy heap on the ground.

And that left one.

The prostrate gunner was unloading at McCarter's muzzle-flashes, short bursts with no precision to them, but he clearly recognized the value of conserving ammunition. Whether he had extra magazines, McCarter had no way of knowing. He could only act on the assumption that his adversary was well armed and bent on pinning him exactly where he was until he caught a break and scored a lucky hit.

The Briton slipped the Browning into its holster and rapidly unslung the AK-47. It was cocked and locked, and a precious second was wasted as he flicked off the safety. McCarter made it twenty feet between himself and the surviving Triad gunner, almost point-blank range.

He waited for a lull between the probing bursts, then leaped from cover on the ''wrong'' side of the tree, away from the position where he had been dueling with his enemies a moment earlier. The gunman tried to compensate, but by the time he shifted to his right, McCarter was already spraying fire from the Kalashnikov, the heavy bullets shredding flesh and fabric as they found their mark.

All done.

The Phoenix Force commando slung the rifle, grabbed the RPG and moved through the trees. He was much closer to the driveway now, and that would mean a straight run toward the house, when he was ready to abandon cover.

The headlights stopped him, two cars appearing from behind the house. It was a pair of limos, which had to mean the big fish were evacuating, with as many troops as they could pack into their cars.

He took a rocket from his satchel, loaded the RPG and braced the launcher on his shoulder, squinting through the sights. The lead car was a hundred feet from where Mc-Carter knelt, still hidden by the trees and darkness, lining up his shot.

The launcher hissed, a fiery comet hurtling across the manicured lawn to keep a date with destiny. It struck the lead car's grille and peeled the hood back, good enough to blind the driver if he wasn't stunned or killed by the initial blast. The car stopped dead, flames boiling from the ruin of its engine, while the driver of the second vehicle stood on his brakes.

McCarter was reloading with his final rocket when the second car reversed, tires smoking on the asphalt drive. He raised the launcher hurriedly, tried lining up the shot, but his elusive quarry was too close to cover, vanishing around a corner of the house and out of sight before he had a chance to fire.

The Briton cursed and sent his last HE round winging toward the house. It plowed through a second-story window and exploded, spewing flames and smoking rubble out into the night.

McCarter dropped the launcher, gripped his AK-47 firmly as he rose and started toward the burning limousine.

IT WAS A FLUKE that Ung Pang was riding in the second car, while Ma Yu rode in the first. It had been Yu's idea to crowd more guns around himself and thus feel more secure. Besides, he had two cars available, and there was

doubtless something in the red pole's stingy nature that re-
belled at leaving either one of them behind.

Dumb luck, and Pang was sitting hunched down in the
back seat of his vehicle, with guards pressed close on either side, when he was startled by the vision of a rocket
streaking from the tree line, reaching out to stop Yu's limo.
A fireball bloomed in the night, the roar of the explosion
audible inside his own car, even with the windows shut.

The driver saved them with his quick reflexes, shifting
into reverse and stomping on the accelerator in the time it
took for Pang to gape and gasp at what had happened to
Ma Yu.

He had to escape, protect himself at any cost. Pang had
a fair jump on that, as it was, the limousine retreating with
a screech of rubber on the pavement, engine racing as they
hurtled back in the direction they had come from. Still not
safe, but rockets didn't fly around corners—unless the enemy was packing cruise missiles—and at least he had a bit
more time to try to save himself.

There seemed to be no other ready exit from the property, at least by car. As soon as they were separated by the
great bulk of the house from their assailant with the rocket
launcher, Pang's wheelman switched off the limo's engine, bailed out of the car and ran back toward the house.
The other gunmen were also unloading in a rush, though
Pang couldn't have said if they had some concerted strategy or if the lot of them had simply fallen prey to panic,
running for their lives.

He shouted at them, trying to assert himself, and even
grabbed one's sleeve before the gunner jerked away and
glared at him, a stream of angry curses pouring from his
lips. That settled any doubts Pang might have had about
their motive: they were fleeing, writing Ma Yu off as a dead
man who could neither help nor harm them anymore. The
last thing any of them wanted at the moment was a brand-
new master most of them had never met before tonight.

Which left Pang on his own, to face the unknown enemy.

He reached inside his jacket and drew the pistol he had tucked into his belt before he came to visit Yu that evening, thumbing back the hammer with a sharp metallic click. If he could find a better weapon, even snatch one from a dead man, Pang would do what had to be done.

He would survive, at any cost.

It was his duty to the People's Revolution, to himself.

The movement needed him, and he wasn't prepared to die.

KATZ FIRED A SHORT BURST from his AK-47, watched his target go down and charged from cover when the way was clear. He didn't know how many gunners Ma Yu had detailed to protect the house, but most of them, as planned, had rallied to the front of the mansion, where McCarter's RPG attack was raising hell and bringing down the house.

The Phoenix Force leader had been staked out on the southwest quadrant of the property, directly opposite McCarter's post, while Bolan moved in from the east. It left one side unmanned, but it was still the best that they could hope for with a three-man strike team.

His task: find Yu and his ChiCom companion, Ung Pang, and kill them. Failing that, inflict as much brute damage on the red pole's home and private army as was possible with the materials at hand. Scorched earth, if necessary, and the tough Israeli knew what that meant, when he met the enemy. No quarter asked or offered.

Everybody died.

Except, if they were very lucky, Katzenelenbogen and his friends.

A swarm of angry hornets buzzed around him, and he hit the deck on knees and elbows, looking for a muzzle-flash to give his enemy away. There he was, on the patio, behind a wrought-iron table that was tilted on its side to make a hasty shield.

Katz rattled off a short burst from his AK-47 and heard the bullets spang off metal. He laid down his rifle and reached back to palm a frag grenade. He hooked the safety pin with one prong of his stainless-steel claw, released it and made the pitch with only minimal delay to calculate the range. It fell a yard left of the mark, bounced once on impact, then began to wobble awkwardly in the direction of his enemy.

The gunner saw it coming and bolted from behind the table. Katz was waiting for him with the AK-47, squeezing off a burst that stopped him dead and pitched him over backward, sprawling into sudden thunder as the hand grenade went off.

He rushed the broad glass doors that fronted on the patio before another enemy could surface and attempt to head him off. A blazing figure eight of bullets cleared the door on Katzenelenbogen's right, and he plunged through it while bright shards of glass were raining to the ground. Unmindful of the small cuts on his scalp and neck, he swept the room in which he found himself, no adversaries visible.

Where should he start to search for Yu and Pang?

As if in answer to the silent question, Katz heard screeching tires outside, from the direction of the driveway that encircled Yu's mansion. Pivoting to face the door where he had lately entered, Katz beheld a limo racing backward, jolting to a halt outside. The doors sprang open, and Chinese gunmen spilled out of the front and back on both sides. He didn't recognize their faces, but it stood to reason that escape vehicles would be limited to persons in authority, and the abortion of their flight meant they were cut off from the street.

Katz saw his opportunity and seized it, charging back outside. He had a better chance of scoring big with whoever waited for him there than if he took the time to search Yu's mansion.

A part of waging war was knowing when to modify your plan and grasp new possibilities, take full advantage of the luck that came your way. Whatever happened in the next few moments, Katz was using his initiative and going for the jugular.

BOLAN WAS ADVANCING on a course designed to intercept the point car, when it suddenly exploded into flame. The rocket from McCarter's RPG slammed through the grille and detonated on the engine block, hot shrapnel driven through the firewall and the dashboard, back into the front seat of the passenger compartment. Doors popped open in the rear, and soldiers started bailing out as flames consumed the vehicle.

He strafed them with his AK-47 and dropped a couple on the run, the others racing back in the direction of the burning house or across the lawn toward darkness that would shelter them from harm...at least until police arrived. A glance inside the limousine, before heat drove him back, and Bolan glimpsed the crumpled form of Ma Yu, slumped in the back seat, where a jagged piece of steel had pierced his forehead, ripping out a fist-sized chunk of skull in back.

The wheelman in the second limousine had wasted no time backing out of there, along the drive and out of sight behind the house. There was no sign of Ung Pang inside the burning car, nor had the runners breaking from it looked familiar. Was he in the second limousine?

The Executioner knew there was only one way to find out.

He ran along the curving asphalt drive, hearing gunfire echoing around the far side of the mansion. One of Bolan's Phoenix Force allies had engaged the enemy, or else Yu's troops were firing blind at shadows. Either way, it served to draw the guns away from Bolan for a moment, and he used the precious time to cover ground.

Around the final corner, he found the second limousine abandoned, doors wide open where the occupants had bailed out in a rush. He saw a pair of Triad gunners, making off toward the garage, and was about to drop them when a sudden movement at the corner of his eye made Bolan pivot, tracking with his AK-47 to acquire a different target.

Yakov Katzenelenbogen flashed a smile and jerked his head back to the right. "He went this way."

"Pang?"

"In the flesh."

They followed him, running side by side across the lawn, the house falling behind them. Trees and darkness loomed ahead, and there was a possibility that they would never find Pang in the woods. Police would be arriving shortly; they would rescue him, examine his credentials and release him to his embassy. The worst that they could do was ship him back to China, protected as he was by the mantle of diplomatic immunity.

It wasn't good enough. Not even close.

Bolan saw the muzzle-flash and dodged to his right. Behind him, Katzenelenbogen grunted and pitched forward on his face. It was impossible to tell if Katz was hit, and there was no time to examine him while they were under fire.

Another flash, the sharp crack of a pistol shot, and Bolan had the gunner marked. He fired a long burst from his AK-47, using more rounds than he would have with a clear-cut target, hosing down the area in case his man jumped to the left or right. There was another pistol shot, but aimless, cranked off to the stars, as if the gunmen had been falling over when he fired.

"Are you all right, Yakov?"

"I'm fine. Just stumbled. Get him!"

Bolan didn't move directly toward the spot where he had seen the last two muzzle-flashes. Rather, he advanced by indirection, circling several yards out of his way to reach the same point, leading with his AK-47, ready to unload on any challengers.

He found Pang sprawled out on his back, one leg bent underneath him at an awkward angle. The man was still alive but fading fast, as much air leaking from the three holes in his chest as from his mouth and nostrils when he breathed. His eyes swam in and out of focus, finally locking onto Bolan's face with sheer determination.

"An American," Pang said.

"What difference does it make?"

"The Dragon will devour you." A pained smile played across his lips, then vanished in a fit of coughing. When he found his voice again, Pang said, "You have no hope."

"We'll see."

He heard Katz coming up behind him, glanced back to make sure, and by the time he turned to face Pang again, the man was dead. He hailed McCarter on the two-way radio, with orders to fall back, and got a swift affirmative. He noticed Katzenelenbogen limping slightly as they moved out toward the trees.

"Sprain something?" Bolan asked.

"A shot of whiskey and I'll be fine," the gruff Israeli told him, but the smile was forced, unnatural.

"I hope so."

"It's in the bag," Katz told him, switching off the smile. "No sweat."

9

Manila

Hop Sung lit a cigarette, drew deeply on it and exhaled smoke through his nostrils. He was bored, the long night dragging on interminably. It reminded him that whorehouse duty, for the bouncers, was a tedious assignment. Working in the strip bars, you could always watch the dancers to amuse yourself, but in a whorehouse it was usual to keep the muscle out of sight in a separate ground-floor room, where he would sit and wait for an alert that one of the establishment's male clients was creating a disturbance.

Such events were rare, but they allowed Sung to break up the monotony with flying fists, a swift kick in the ass for some pathetic idiot who couldn't manage to control himself. Sung liked it better when the idiots were round-eyes, flabby tourists or some fresh-faced sailor from a U.S. Navy ship parked in Manila Bay. It was a pleasure, using muscle on the white men when he had a chance.

But not tonight.

His shift was almost over. He would be relieved soon, free to leave, another evening wasted watching television and drinking beer.

Still, it was better than a real job, sweating in the sun for wages that would barely keep a mouse alive. Sung knew he should be thankful, but he **still** longed for some action.

The sudden rapping on his door surprised him, made him jump. He frowned and scrambled to his feet. Since when did they start knocking when they needed him?

Sung opened up the door... and froze.

A white man stood before him, tall and dark, well-dressed. The automatic pistol in his hand was aimed at Sung's face, the muzzle looking twice its normal size up close. The Triad hardman considered reaching for his weapon, then imagined what would happen if the round-eye's gun went off six inches from his skull. He had a mental flash of brains spilled on the floor and knew it wasn't worth the risk.

The man spoke to him in English. "Let me see the gun."

It crossed Sung's mind to make believe he didn't speak the language, try to stall for time, but what would that achieve? He might provoke the stranger into violent action, sacrifice himself, and all for what? Some whores?

Sung pulled back the left side of his jacket, made no effort to obstruct the white man as he reached out with his free hand and removed Sung's pistol.

"You need to get this place cleared out," the stranger said. "Three minutes, one way or another, and it's going up in smoke."

Sung blinked, not fully understanding the demand at first, but then he glanced beyond the stranger, saw a canvas satchel in the hall behind him propped against the wall. Explosives? An incendiary? He didn't know or care, and nodded comprehension, moving only when his captor stepped aside to let him pass.

There was a fire alarm a few steps from the door of Sung's waiting room. The stranger had to have seen it but he had chosen not to pull the lever, stopping first to confront the bouncer. Sung glanced back at the gunman, reaching for the lever, and the white man merely nodded, giving him the go-ahead. An instant later the alarm was clamoring, Sung could hear the girls and patrons rushing from their rooms upstairs.

It was a sight to see, most of them naked, several of the customers with clothing bundled in their arms. They jammed together at the exit, jostling one another, cursing, finally clearing out.

When they were gone, the white man said, "Okay, you're done."

It struck Sung that he was free to leave, then he thought of Hwak Tan and the questions he would have to answer from his red pole if he fled the whorehouse without putting up a fight. He had allowed himself to be disarmed, humiliated by a round-eye. There would be no mercy for him when he turned in his report. Better to take a bullet in the head, he thought, than to face punishment that was protracted over days.

Sung made his move, a rush that would have taken most men by surprise. He waited for the bullet, but didn't understand why he was still alive. Then the white man clubbed him with the pistol in his right hand, followed with a hard chop from the weapon in his left. Sung went down on his face, blood streaming from a scalp wound and a gash below one eye. His ears were ringing, and he felt his supper coming back to haunt him in a greasy rush of bile.

When he was finished retching, Sung glanced up and found the white man crouching at his side.

"Feel better now?" the stranger asked.

Sung thought about it, dripping blood, and nodded.

"Fair enough. You've got about one minute to get out of here, unless you want to fry." Then he was gone.

Sung scrambled to his feet and raced toward the nearest exit. He was in the street when white smoke started pouring from the brothel, spreading like a fog bank as it reached the open air.

He was alive, with wounds to prove that he had done his job—or tried to. His superiors could ask no more.

Sung hoped not, anyway.

The bloodied Triad soldier started looking for a phone booth, wishing he could turn the clock back, find himself inside the whorehouse once again. Still bored. Still safe.

THE MAIN STREET of Manila's Chinatown, Ongpin, in the old Binondo district, was more or less deserted at the midnight hour, shops and hole-in-the-wall factories closed for the night, their owners and employees long since home in bed. The workday started early for Manila's Chinese residents, and it was still the middle of the week, no time for relaxation.

Mack Bolan was a half mile from the burned-out brothel when he found the address he was looking for—a walk-up office with the stairs outside. Nobody was there to greet him at the moment, but it made no difference to his plan.

There would be time enough for facing soldiers when they had a foothold in Manila. Right now he was interested in getting the attention of a certain gangster who had ruled the roost in Chinatown for close to fifteen years. One way to wake him up and get the new day off to a bad start was torching property his target owned. Let him enjoy the taste of ashes in his mouth, while Bolan and his comrades launched the next phase of their campaign in the Philippines.

He climbed the stairs and drew a penlight from his pocket, checking out the office door. There was no burglar alarm because the residents of Chinatown knew who owned the property, and none of them would challenge Hwak Tan. The red pole was, if not a god, at least a minor legend to his people, with a reputation for ferocity that made potential enemies think twice, at least, before they took him on.

He could have picked the lock, but didn't care to waste the time. A swift kick cleared his way, and Bolan stepped across the threshold, confident, without a weapon in his hand. The darkness told him there would be no watchman. He had all the time he needed to complete his business here.

The first desk on his right would normally be occupied by a receptionist. He left his satchel there, removed a pair of fat incendiary canisters and walked back to the red pole's private office. Tan hadn't seen fit to lock the door, so certain was he of his own invincibility. The file cabinets and his desk *were* locked, but Bolan didn't care. The thermite would burn through them like a blowtorch melting butter once the fire broke out.

He pulled the pins on both incendiary bombs, rolled one beneath Tan's desk and tossed the other one between two file cabinets in the southeast corner of the room. One bomb would certainly have done the trick, but he had plenty, and he wasn't taking any chances. Passing through the outer office on his way back to the exit, Bolan dropped one more and left it sputtering.

The loss of property and records would be nothing critical to Tan, a lifelong criminal who made his living from the misery of addicts and compulsive gamblers, but the very fact of being challenged in his private fiefdom might unnerve him. At the very least, it had to make him stop and think—about his future prospects of survival, and the wisdom of his master's personal decision to cooperate with agents from Beijing.

Bolan waited in an alley across the street to make sure that the thermite did its job. It was unlikely the Manila fire brigade would have the proper chemicals on hand when they responded to the first alarm, and by the time they had corrected their mistake, the place would be a total loss. With Katzenelenbogen and McCarter on the job, as well, he could inflict substantial damage on Tan before the red pole even knew he had an enemy in town.

And by the time he realized his peril, it would be too late.

Bolan scratched the office from his mental hit list as he walked back to the side street where he had parked his rented compact car. He had other stops to make before the sun rose on Manila to inaugurate another day, and time was always short in the Executioner's world.

He lived on borrowed time, in fact had since the first day of his private holy war against the savages, and he could never tell exactly when he might be called upon to pay that cosmic debt. The only thing he knew for certain was that standing still meant wasting time, and that was tantamount to giving up.

He was well away and rolling in the compact by the time he heard the sirens closing on the site of Tan's former business office. Too late, already, but he wished them luck.

The Executioner had other fish to fry.

THE CLUB on Roxas Boulevard stayed open until sunrise, catering to an exclusive clientele. It was the kind of place where foreign diplomats rubbed shoulders with the upper crust of Filipino politics and enterprise. Unknown to the majority of foreign visitors—and many natives, too—the club was owned by Hwak Tan. He called it the Flamingo, after Bugsy Siegel's old casino in Las Vegas, and the red pole took great pride in his ability to move among the men and women who defined "Society."

McCarter drove behind the club, ignoring the valets out front, and went in through the back. The door was open there, because the kitchen help made frequent garbage runs to containers in the parking lot.

McCarter ran a gauntlet of employees as he entered, all in sweaty kitchen whites. They looked him up and down, but no one made a move to block his path. The Uzi in his hand persuaded them that it wouldn't be wise to interfere with this grim visitor, and by the time he reached the dining room of the Flamingo, most of them had vanished through the back door.

Just as well.

He didn't need some dishwasher or fry cook trying to impress the boss by coming at him with a cleaver when he went to leave. McCarter hadn't come to the Flamingo to shoot kitchen workers, but that wouldn't stop him, either, if they tried to do him harm.

The main room of the club was spacious, with a small stage for musicians in the southwest corner, a parquet dance floor near the stage and room for ninety or a hundred tables that would seat four in a pinch, if no one minded rubbing knees. Perhaps two-thirds of those were occupied by couples now, most of the women noticeably younger than their escorts, many of them Filipinos dining with older Europeans or Americans.

McCarter didn't give a damn about their sex lives, and a part of him was sorry that he had to spoil their evening, but he had a job to do.

The band was playing loud enough that it would make no sense for him to give a verbal warning, so he swung up the Uzi and raked the ceiling with a burst of twelve or thirteen rounds. Fluorescent lighting fixtures burst and sprinkled powdered glass on startled patrons, as the music died.

"Go home!" McCarter shouted to his captive audience. "The club is closing for repairs!"

He didn't have to tell them twice. It was a stampede for the exits, no one coming any closer to McCarter than they had to in the rush. He waited for the soldiers, knowing they had to be there somewhere, tucked away from public view. He was ready when a door flew open near the stage and three young Chinese emerged in response to sounds of gunfire.

There was no one between McCarter and his adversaries when they burst into the main room of the club. He had already marked the door as it began to open and had the Uzi sighted, his finger tightening around the trigger, waiting only to be sure how many guns were ranged against him. When he understood that there were only three,

McCarter closed his mind to anything but duty, holding down the trigger on his SMG and riddling them with parabellum slugs before they even knew where the destructive fire was coming from.

He stood alone, reloading, waiting for a second wave, but there were no more guns to challenge him. Not yet. If he stood waiting long enough, no doubt police or reinforcements from the 14K would soon arrive, but he wasn't an idiot. The job he had to do would take another sixty seconds, maybe less, and then he would be gone.

Removing thermite canisters from the deep pockets of his raincoat, he considered that there might be some employees hiding somewhere in the club. There was no time to search for them, but he would give them one more warning, just in case.

"Get out!" he shouted to the empty room. "The club is burning down!"

That done, he primed the thermite bombs, tossed one behind the bar and lobbed the other into the middle of the room. He was almost to the exit when he heard them detonate, the reek of chemicals and smoke pursuing him outside.

Manila had a reputation as a hot town with the servicemen who passed that way, as well as countless visitors each year who purchased "sex tours" from their travel agents. There were different kinds of heat, though, just as there were different kinds of passion.

A brand-new fire was being kindled in Manila, and the place would never be the same again.

THE TRUCKING COMPANY, with headquarters in the Ermita district of Manila, was another property of Hwak Tan. As a "legitimate" investment, it allowed him to report substantial income for taxation, even while the trucks at his command transported contraband from time to time. They ferried prostitutes, narcotics, weapons, stolen goods, illegal aliens. A number of them had lately been "hijacked" and appropriated by left-wing guerrillas waging war against the Filipino government, a circumstance the CIA regarded as no mere coincidence, since leaders of the 14K had made their devil's bargain with the plotters in Beijing.

In any case, the trucks would have to go, and there was no time for a bit of surgery like the small hours prior to dawn, with Tan's employees off the property.

Katz braced the Russian RPG across his shoulder, peering through the sights to choose his first mark from the line of trucks that stood outside a combination warehouse and garage. His perch atop the flat roof of another warehouse, facing Tan's establishment, permitted him to aim without the need of firing through a chain-link fence that ringed the property.

He had counted thirteen diesel rigs lined up across the blacktop parking lot, against one rocket in the RPG and three more lined up on the roof beside him. Speed was a consideration, but the hour made him less concerned with an immediate police response than if it had been noon, or even earlier at night. The rapid-fire explosions would attract attention, certainly, but by the time their source was isolated and alarms were raised, Katz would be on the way to his next target.

Working systematically, he chose the far truck on his left, at one end of the line, and sent his first shot winging off toward impact on a tail of fire. The blast stung Katzenelenbogen's ears, but he was well beyond the range of heat and flying shrapnel on his rooftop perch. He had the second rocket loaded by the time the shock wave reached him, pushing muggy air in front of it, and lined up on the far truck to his right.

Round two bored through the diesel's grille, the tall cab rearing rising on a cloud of smoke and fire. The fuel tank went up in a secondary blast as he was loading rocket number three and lining up another shot.

Round three went to the middle truck in line, a blast that spattered burning fuel on vehicles to either side, sent shrapnel winding up and down the line. A lake of burning oil and diesel fuel had spread beneath the trucks, flames licking at the others, melting tires and searching for the fuel lines, heating metal to the point where liquids boiled or burned and paint was scorched away.

One rocket remained, and Katzenelenbogen didn't care to waste it on the burning vehicles. Instead, he sighted on the building. Squeezing off, he watched the missile punch through brittle glass and disappear, its fiery tail illuminating the warehouse interior for a second and a half before it blew. God only knew what Tan had stored in there, but it was burning fiercely by the time Katz made his way down to the street and stowed his launcher in the hatchback of his rental car, concealed by blankets and an OD duffel bag.

Manila would be waking up before much longer, and the dawn would bring grim news to Hwak Tan. Katz felt refreshed, despite the scant amount of sleep he had enjoyed between departure from Cambodia and their arrival in the Philippines. Not rested, in the normal sense, but more rejuvenated. They were moving toward the climax of their mission, and he would be there at the finish line, regardless of fatigue or the misgivings that he felt inside. It had been touch and go around Phnom Penh, but he was feeling better now. More confident.

And if he failed, it wouldn't be from lack of trying. No one, in the end, would say that he had quit his post or broken faith.

Katz was pledged to the fight and would follow it through.

To the end of the line.

THE PLASTIQUE CHARGE weighed seven pounds. It was enough to leave a large apartment house in ruins, if applied correctly, but the Executioner's target was considerably smaller. The saloon on Quezon Boulevard was yet another property of Hwak Tan's, closed and deserted in the predawn hours. A popular watering hole for locals and foreign servicemen alike, it featured prostitutes and covert drug sales in addition to the booze and naked dancers that were its legitimate attractions. Once again, the business let Tan show a source of income for taxation purposes, while washing dirty cash and giving him a place to deal with customers who came in search of something more than alcohol.

The back door had been wired for an alarm, and there was no way of knowing whether it connected to police or Tan's own soldiers. Either way, the moment Bolan broke that circuit, he would be in danger of a rude surprise from men with guns. He had no qualms about his own ability to hit and run before the cavalry arrived, but there was more to think about than simply dropping off his charge and bailing out.

From the beginning of his one-man war, the Executioner had pledged that he would never kill a cop, regardless of the circumstances. Some of them were criminals and murderers with badges, granted, but his private vow remained inviolate. He wouldn't drop the hammer on a lawman, nor would he bait traps that put police in killing situations.

Bolan knelt and placed his satchel on the ground, reset the timer for a maximum of ninety seconds. There were no prowl cars in the immediate vicinity—he had assured himself of that before he made his move—and a police response from any greater distance in a minute and a half was physically impossible. The narrow margin made it still more difficult for Bolan to escape before the bomb went off, but he would have to take that chance.

To save some time, he left the lock picks in his pocket, gave the door a solid kick to snap the lock and shouldered through to darkness. No alarm was audible, but he could hear the doomsday numbers running all the same. He put the satchel down, opened it, found the arming button and pressed it. The red light winked at him as he closed the flap and turned back toward the doorway.

Bolan hit the alley running and turned left, racing toward his car one hundred feet away. He made it, slid behind the wheel and twisted the ignition key. The engine roared to life as an explosion shook the block, one noise eclipsing and devouring the other. He was rolling as the first flames spilled into the alley, bits and pieces of the shattered structure raining within a radius of several hundred feet.

Hard times were coming for the 14K, and Hwak Tan would know it soon. The fat was in the fire, and blood debts long deferred were being called in.

He wasn't certain yet where Tan and his Manila family fit into Beijing's dealings with the 14K, but he would know before he left the city and put the Philippines behind him. And he meant to bring the family down, by any means available.

"The Dragon will devour you."

A prophecy, or mere bravado?

Bolan couldn't say, and it wouldn't have changed his plans in either case. One dragon or another had been trying to devour him for years, without success. If he had let the fear of sudden death prevent him from continuing, his war would have been over on day one.

That he had come this far was testament to Bolan's courage and determination. What transpired within the next few hours or days would be a testament to his survival skills.

10

Raoul Ramos left his car on Roxas Boulevard and started walking north toward Rizal Park. He had time before his meeting with the stranger, but he wanted to arrive before the other man and have a look around the park to make sure that he wasn't blundering into a trap.

For nearly thirteen years Ramos had been leading what was often called a double—or a triple—life. A peasant who had gravitated toward the Filipino capital when he was still a teen, Ramos had drifted into crime and faced imprisonment for his conviction on a residential burglary before police had offered him a choice. The charges would be set aside, they said, on manufactured technicalities, if Ramos would agree to feed them information on the vast Manila underworld. He had agreed with some misgivings, and discovered that he had a knack for spying, worming information out of men who should know better, covering his tracks so that the cold, accusing finger never pointed in his direction.

Over time, he had acquired a reputation with police detectives in Manila for the accuracy of his information and the cases that were broken with his aid. Word got around, through certain channels, and an agent of the CIA approached him two years later, offering substantial payments if Ramos would broaden his investigations into the political arena, keeping watch on certain groups described as left-wing, Communist, anti-American. He accepted the proposal, and his transformation from a sneak thief into a Filipino James Bond was complete.

In seven years of working for the CIA, this morning marked the third time he had been required to meet a contact in the flesh. Most often he used mail drops, writing information by hand on notebook paper, sealing it in envelopes and leaving it at designated places, to be read by people he would never see. The last two times a meeting was required, to relay complicated orders, Ramos wound up talking to the same man who recruited him to serve the Company. This day, though, he was made to understand that it would be a stranger, someone trustworthy but dangerous if crossed.

Ramos was troubled, entering the park and moving slowly toward the Rizal monument, a statue honoring a Filipino martyr executed in the nineteenth century. It made no sense to him that this should be a trap—why would the Company endanger him for no good reason?—but he was nervous all the same. He had a pistol underneath his baggy peasant shirt, with which he could defend himself if all else failed. Ramos hoped it wouldn't come to that, but life was more important to him than his secret job, and he would fight if necessary.

They had given him a rough description of the man he was supposed to meet: American, something over six feet tall, dark hair, around two hundred pounds. He would be carrying a camera case—not wearing it around his neck, as tourists often did—but holding it in his left hand.

To keep the right hand free for shooting? Ramos wondered, sorry that the thought had crossed his mind.

He checked his own gun unobtrusively as he approached the statue, circled wide around it, dawdling in the sun.

A stranger was approaching, tall by Filipino standards, passing Ramos without a second glance. The informant took note of hair, height, weight, the leather camera case this stranger carried in his left hand, with the thin strap wound around his knuckles. Moving past the statue, Mr. X picked out an empty bench and sat at one end of it. His empty right hand rested on his thigh, where it could make a rapid move inside the dark, unbuttoned sport coat.

Armed? Why not? Who wasn't packing weapons in the Philippines these days?

Ramos drifted toward the bench, prepared to flee or fight at the first sign of danger. He would play along as far as possible, see what the stranger wanted, but he wouldn't sacrifice himself for strangers. His life hadn't come to that.

Reluctantly, with cautious strides, he closed in on the bench and sat at the far end from his contact, waiting.

IN NORMAL CIRCUMSTANCES, Hwak Tan slept in until nine o'clock most mornings, read his newspaper with breakfast and was ready to begin his working day by 10:30 a.m. By nine o'clock this morning, though, he had been wide-awake for nearly five hours. Breakfast had been coffee and a pastry he couldn't remember tasting, while he worked the telephones and tried to find out what was happening around Manila, who dared to attack him in this way.

There had been seven incidents since 3:15 a.m., and precious time had slipped away while his subordinates were arguing about the wisdom of disturbing him at home. Three soldiers were dead and seven properties destroyed, including bars and brothels, his trucking company, the very office where he spent a portion of his time each weekday, signing checks and shuffling papers at an antique desk.

All gone.

The anger made Tan clench his fists, but he knew well enough that rage alone would get him nowhere in his search for enemies. The kind of damage he had suffered overnight could only mean his foes were organized, well armed and bent on ruining his family. It might have helped to know their motives, but Tan was more concerned with names.

It felt like waking from a nightmare to discover that your gruesome dream world was reality. Tan was aware of the events in Burma, Thailand and Cambodia that had left his brothers dead or fleeing for their lives. He had decided that no one would surprise him and had posted guards, but it had seemed unlikely that the round-eyes would take time to raid the Philippines when they were so close to the hill chief in Hong Kong. If they were waging all-out war against the 14K, what better than to kill the man in charge, create a void of leadership?

It had occurred to Tan, before the trouble started in his own backyard, that a replacement for the hill chief would be necessary, when he went to join his ancestors. The job required a man of skill, intelligence, experience, with proven managerial abilities. Who better than the oldest red pole in the 14K, who had been running operations in the Philippines for fifteen years without a major hitch?

Until today.

Tan's dream was slipping through his fingers. The only way to save it was for him to isolate and kill the men who had embarrassed him, destroyed so many of his comrades in the past two weeks. Once that was done, he would be in an excellent position to demand a greater voice in family affairs. And when the hill chief shuffled off to paradise, perhaps with some assistance from a faithful friend to get him started, Hwak Tan would be the heir apparent to his throne.

But first he had to prove himself once more, deal with the men who had confounded red poles, slaughtered Triad soldiers. And it began with personal humiliation, phoning his report to Edward Wong before some other, equally ambitious member of the clan could tip off the hill chief to Tan's embarrassment. Unpleasant work was best done personally to make sure you got it right the first time, with no need to repeat the job or counteract the misconceptions circulated by false friends.

His spies and soldiers had Manila covered now. Too late to keep the fire from spreading, possibly, but any further outbreaks would be spotted swiftly, hopefully contained by flying squads of skilled assassins. Tan would call on Wong Kam if he had to and recruit guerrillas from the rural provinces, but that would be a last resort. A warning should suffice, for now, to put the mainland diplomat on guard and make him watch his step.

Tan, meanwhile, had soldiers to direct, a war to supervise. His enemy had an advantage at the moment, but the red pole knew how quickly that could change. One sighting, one small piece of information that would put him on their track, and Tan would make his adversaries wish that they were never born.

It galled Tan that he could only sit and wait for some word from the streets. He felt as if he should be out there doing something, but his rank and circumstance had relegated him to sitting like a spider in the center of his web, waiting for a tasty insect to disturb the clutching strands of silk.

Tan was adept at waiting, though. It was another of his skills, which friends and enemies alike were prone to underestimate.

One day, before too long, the red pole of Manila would surprise them all.

Macau

THE NEWS WAS BAD, but Cheung Kuo expected nothing less. The past two weeks had helped remind him that adversity was part of life. He had already learned that lesson, growing up in China, but it never hurt to have important knowledge reinforced. Kuo told himself it was a growth experience, something to keep him humble, but the platitudes rang hollow.

Kuo was more concerned with victory and loss just now, the rudiments of personal survival in a system where mistakes were often viewed as willful negligence, and failure was rewarded by demotion, exile or a bullet in the head. Kuo hadn't reached that point as yet, but there was no doubt his superiors were starting to regret approval of his plan to use the Triads as an adjunct of their covert foreign policy.

Survival called for him to turn the trend around. The bad news from the Philippines came hard on top of the disaster in Cambodia, but now the Dragon told himself that it might be a blessing in disguise. His apparatus in the archipelago was powerful, well organized, and he had gained a similar impression of the 14K. The Chinese gangsters had been doing business form Manila, Cebu and Davao since World War II, if not before. Their roots were deep in Filipino soil, and they had powerful connections with the government, despite the fall of one corrupt regime, replaced by something hardly better where the working people were concerned.

The call had come from Edward Wong, immediately followed by another from Wong Kam, himself established in Manila. Their assessments of the problem were essentially identical: their adversaries in the Philippines had to be associated with the men responsible for previous attacks across three continents, if they weren't the same terrorists—Americans, beyond a reasonable doubt, and probably supported by the CIA or some such agency in Washington.

Which told the Dragon nothing that he couldn't have decided on his own. The hill chief and Kam were covering themselves, of course, unloading the responsibility on him, but Kuo was used to that. His rank came with responsibility attached, and he wasn't a man to slough off his duties onto others. He would deal with those who tried to bring him down . . . if only he could find out who and where they were.

Manila offered countless hiding places for a fugitive, but these men were aggressive, eager to confront their chosen enemies. It was inevitable that they expose themselves in order to pursue their grand crusade. And when they surfaced next, the Dragon's allies would be waiting for them.

He would eat them up alive.

Or so he hoped, at any rate.

Another loss wouldn't sit well with his superiors, nor would it help the hill chief of the 14K to pacify his worried troops. The last thing Kuo needed was a civil war within the Triad he had chosen as his vehicle for spreading Chinese influence around the world. He understood the mind of Edward Wong, could work with him for common benefits, but Wong's successor might be less accommodating to Beijing. In fact, if he suspected that collaboration was the cause of all their difficulties, a replacement might reject the bargain altogether.

Kuo couldn't permit that to occur. He knew what it would mean for him, and he wasn't prepared to let some devious provincial gangster scuttle his career. If necessary, he would take a hand himself to keep Wong on his throne as hill chief and prevent his plan from going down the toilet.

No Saint George had yet appeared to make this Dragon quake in fear. Kuo still had tricks he hadn't used, but it was almost time to use them.

He smiled and reached out for the telephone.

Manila

RAMOS PLACED a cigarette between his lips and turned to Bolan, asking, "Do you have a match?"

"I use a lighter," Bolan answered.

"Better still," the Filipino said.

"Until they go wrong."

The exchange smacked of something from an old spy novel, but it did the trick. He leaned across the bench to light the cigarette, wondering if the Company brains took their codes from pulp fiction or paid someone to dream them up from scratch.

It didn't matter. He had contact now, and it was time to get to work.

"You come highly recommended," Bolan said to break the ice.

Ramos smiled. "I hope I live up to the advertising."

"One way to find out. You have a name?"

"Raoul."

"I'm Mike."

"What is it that you want from me today?"

"I'm working on a problem that involves the Triads and the Red Chinese."

Raoul blinked once, then blew twin jets of smoke through his nostrils. "You wouldn't, by any chance, be one of those responsible for several incidents this morning? The destruction of substantial property belonging to a certain Chinese businessman?"

"Suppose I am?"

"You have my admiration, sir," Ramos replied, "and my sincere best wishes. You will need the help of God Himself, I think."

"Right now," Bolan said, "I'd be satisfied with information."

"By all means. The Communists and Triads are no friends of mine."

"I understand the Reds have been supplying left-wing rebels in the rural provinces. Guerrilla fighters who oppose the government."

"That's true enough," Ramos agreed. "It's said a Chinese diplomat called Wong Kam is a close friend of the strongest red pole in Manila, Hwak Tan. They dine together now and then, but the police have no hard evidence connecting Tan with the guerrillas. And, of course, he pays some of them very well to look the other way."

"My understanding is that you know the leader of the rebels," Bolan said.

"I know *of* him. It's very different, you'll agree, than knowing him. His name isn't a secret, though you seldom see it in the press these days."

"Fidel Aristo," Bolan said.

"The very same."

"I want to meet him."

Ramos was frowning as he dropped his cigarette and crushed it beneath his heel. "A Yankee? That won't be possible."

"They tell me you work wonders."

"They are wrong," the Filipino said.

"Suppose there was a reason for the meeting? Suppose Aristo wanted to explore new options, with his Chinese backers on the ropes?"

"New options?"

"Someone who can keep the weapons coming, even if Beijing bows out."

"A mercenary proposition?"

"Call it anything you like. I need to reel him in, a one-shot deal. Just bring him close enough that I can get him in the net."

Ramos considered it. At last he said, "There are ways to communicate with him, of course."

"I thought so."

"It would be a risky proposition—no less for the messenger than for yourself."

"If it works out the way I'm hoping," Bolan said, "Fidel won't be in any shape to order a reprisal. If I blow it, then the messenger should try a change of scene."

"Such relocation is expensive," Ramos reminded him.

The envelope in Bolan's inside pocket was an inch thick, stuffed with crisp new hundred-dollar bills. It came to fifteen thousand dollars, give or take.

"That ought to get you started," Bolan said.

"My homeland—"

"Will no doubt be grateful for your services, if you can help me wrap this up."

Ramos weighed the money in his hand. "And if you are successful? Then what?"

"Keep the money, with my compliments. Consider it a tip."

There was no point in telling him the cash had been converted into U.S. dollars from the Triad's war chest, money lifted from his raids on several covert banks in Europe ten days earlier.

"I have some contacts in Manila," Ramos allowed. "They can relay a message to Aristo but don't speak for him. You understand? I cannot guarantee that he will meet with you."

"I'll take the chance," Bolan said. "While he thinks it over, I suspect his Chinese friends have got some bad luck coming."

"More bad luck?" Ramos smiled and shook his head.

The Executioner smiled with him. "When it rains, it pours."

"So, you're familiar with our weather in the Philippines."

"I get my feet wet, every now and then."

"You may need more than an umbrella this time," Ramos stated.

"I always come prepared."

The little man didn't look convinced, but he was calm enough to shrug and make the money disappear. "I will do what I can," he said. "Where can I reach you?"

"I don't have a number at the moment. You'd better give me yours."

Ramos was visibly reluctant to divulge the number, but the money in his pocket made it somewhat easier. "What I must do needs several hours," he told Bolan. "Call me sometime after one o'clock this afternoon. I have no answering machine, but I will wait at home when I am finished with our business."

"Fair enough."

The Filipino rose to leave, but something made him hesitate. "Forgive my asking this—are you a man of faith?"

"I never thought about it much," the Executioner replied.

Ramos nodded his understanding. "I have always thought my business would displease God, if there *is* a God. My parents were believers, though. Sometimes I still feel moved to ask for help."

"It couldn't hurt," Bolan said.

"No. There may, perhaps, be blessings even for the likes of you and me."

With that, the man turned away and ambled off across the park, while Bolan headed in the opposite direction. He had no idea if Ramos could fix a meeting with Fidel Aristo, but the 14K was paying for it, either way. If it worked out, he had a shot at taking down the rebel hierarchy with a single stroke; if not, well, he would simply have to do the job some other way.

There were more ways than one to skin a cat . . . or slay a Dragon.

The monster was already wounded, but it wasn't finished yet. Before the final death blow was delivered, Bolan had to sap his adversary's strength some more. Every blow he struck against the Dragon now improved the chances of survival for himself and his associates. When they reached the serpent's nest, if they got that far, the enemy would be disoriented, weakened, handicapped by fear.

Or so he hoped.

Bolan turned and started walking back toward his car.

WONG KAM FELT BETTER after speaking to the Dragon. Not relaxed, but more at ease than he had been when Hwak Tan called him at home that morning to tell him that Manila was besieged. They were no closer to discovering their enemies, but Kam had no end of confidence. He would prevail, with some assistance from Tan, because the People's Revolution wouldn't be denied.

Kam's first step was to reach out for Fidel Aristo. It wasn't a simple thing to reach the rebel leader, down on Mindanao, but Kam had contacts, people he could trust to carry messages. Aristo would call him back sometime that day, or possibly the next. When they spoke, Kam would arrange for the guerrillas to be mobilized on two fronts simultaneously. In Manila, they would help Tan in his pursuit of the elusive enemy. Meanwhile, outside the capital, Aristo's soldiers would renew their drive against the government, distracting Filipino troops and demonstrating, through a classic show of force, that they weren't intimidated by a few Americans who dropped in for the weekend to attack the 14K.

They had been lucky so far, these adventurers who thought they had a chance of stopping history—or fate, as it was called by those who put their trust in forces outside humankind. The tide was turning, though; their luck was running out. They were moving toward a confrontation with a grim, clandestine warrior who had never given ground before his enemies.

And he wouldn't be starting now.

11

Davao, Mindanao

Raoul Ramos had arranged a meeting between "Mike Belasko," a renegade American arms dealer, and Fidel Aristo, current leader of the left-wing insurrectionists who had been raising hell throughout the Philippines for more than a decade. Fond of Russian hardware before the Soviet Union collapsed and the Berlin Wall came down, the rebels had no qualms about accepting aid from the Chinese— or anybody else who could support their war. When it came down to buying weapons, Bolan understood, Aristo's army managed to support its habit through armed robbery, extortion, ransom kidnappings and the occasional murder for hire. The rebels might despise Americans, but they would listen to his sales pitch, think about it, ponder the alternatives.

Except that Bolan wasn't in Davao to make a sale. He had instructed Ramos to set the meet as a convenient way of making contact with Aristo. There would be no sales pitch, no protracted haggling over prices. Once he had the target in his sights, with Katzenelenbogen and McCarter backing him, the Executioner would strike.

With any luck, it should work out all right.

Unless the meet proved to be a trap.

He had considered that risk from the start, and it was on his mind as Bolan locked his car, then walked north along a side street toward the park that was supposed to be their meeting place. In deference to the weather and appearances, he wore a baggy peasant shirt, with two Beretta automatic pistols underneath, where he could reach them in a rush. The pockets of his trousers sagged with extra magazines.

The others should be well in place by now. He didn't bother to look for them as he reached the park. If they had done their jobs correctly, they would be invisible.

He found a bench and waited, small hairs bristling on his nape as if a sniper's telescopic sight were focused there. No bullet came, though, and he killed five minutes waiting by himself before the first of two cars came in view, approaching from the east. As both drew closer, he could see that they were full of men, presumably all armed and dangerous. He counted ten and wondered whether there were more, concealed on the perimeter perhaps, or waiting in another vehicle, just out of sight.

It was too late to think about it now.

The Executioner sat back and waited for the action to begin.

FIDEL ARISTO HAD LISTENED respectfully to Wong Kam's warning, told the Chinaman that he would use discretion if he was approached by any strangers in the next few days. Aristo saw no need to mention that he had already been approached, albeit indirectly, by a Yankee arms dealer. It would be foolish—not to mention dangerous—for him to tell the Red Chinese that he had thoughts of dealing with their enemies to purchase military hardware that wasn't available from Beijing.

Aristo was a revolutionary socialist, but he wasn't committed at all costs to Maoist dogma, as the Chinese seemed to be, behind their smiling mask of economic trade-offs with the West. If an American could sell him weapons to defeat the very government admired by Washington, so much the better. As an educated man, Aristo had an eye for irony.

He saw the stranger from a block away, a solitary white man lounging on the bench, decked out in peasant shirt and khaki trousers. Tourist clothes. He had no briefcase or valise that would contain a weapon larger than a handgun, but that baggy shirt could hide a multitude of sins.

Aristo reached beneath his own shirt and gave the big Colt .45 a reassuring love pat. He was ready, and his men were armed with automatic weapons, shotguns, anything a flying squad would need to shoot its way out of a trap, if such this proved to be.

And if this stranger was a mortal enemy, it would have been sheer cowardice to hide from him. Whatever else Fidel Aristo was, whatever he had done or had his soldiers do, no one among his enemies in government had ever claimed he had a yellow streak.

Aristo left his car and waited for his soldiers to fan out behind him. Only two of them would join him on his walk across the open grass, the others hanging back, prepared to move if anything went wrong. The rebel leader glanced around the area and was satisfied with what he saw.

Control.

Coupled with firepower, it was the only rule that mattered on a battlefield. Control was everything.

The warm sun baked into Aristo's back and shoulders as he went to meet the stranger from America. Whatever happened in the next few moments, he had done all he could to prepare himself.

The rest, he thought, was up to fate.

McCARTER LAY CONCEALED in the undergrowth, sixty yards due west of Bolan's bench. The park attendants evidently didn't spend much time on clearing ferns and brush around the fringes of the park, and he was thankful for their negligence. If they had been more conscientious, he would have been forced to share the public washroom with Katzenelenbogen, and their layout for a cross fire would have gone to hell.

This way, he got to use the RPG. Its first blast would betray him, let the rebels pinpoint his location, but by that time it would be too late. Instead of checking out the trap and giving it a miss, they would be forced to fight their way clear under fire.

Those who survived the first few moments, anyway.

He wished Aristo's men had lingered in the cars, more concentrated targets for the missile that would start the killing party, but McCarter was experienced enough to work with what he had. At that, three of the eight men who remained spread out behind Aristo waited near the lead car, probably the drivers and an extra gun to keep them company if the police turned up or anything necessitated swift evacuation from the scene.

McCarter made it close to eighty yards, still child's play for the RPG. He sighted on the lead car's right-front fender, fixing his point of impact between two gunners who were standing awkwardly beside the car, shirts bulging with the hardware hidden underneath.

The rocket hissed downrange and rocked the point car like a bullet ripping through a child's toy. The gunners closest to the blast died instantly, engulfed by flame and torn by shrapnel, cheated of the opportunity to scream, much less defend themselves. Their comrade on the far side of the vehicle sprawled over backward out of sight and didn't rise again. Between the shrapnel, the shock wave and the spreading lake of fire that blazed around the car, McCarter reckoned he was done.

Well-done, in fact.

Chaos ensued as the guerrillas drew their weapons and opened fire on anything that moved, while Bolan made a dive for cover, pistols filling his hands.

McCarter still had work to do before he laid the RPG aside and picked up his Kalashnikov. He was assigned to make sure that the rebels had no rapid means of exit from the park, which meant he had to blow the other car—and soon, before their adversaries started thinking clearly and began a mass retreat.

He aimed, squeezed off and watched the second car disintegrate. The pool of flaming gasoline immediately doubled, black smoke blotting out a corner of the bright blue sky.

The Briton reached out for his rifle then, and wedged the folding metal stock against his shoulder, sighting down the barrel as the rebels still in any shape to fight converged on Bolan, firing as they came.

"Come on," he whispered. "Come and get it!"

BOLAN WAS READY when the RPG rocket came out of right field, sizzling across his line of vision, rocking the point car like a giant fist of smoke and flame. He ripped three buttons from his shirt as he was grabbing for his guns, Aristo and the others understanding that it was a trap and drawing weapons of their own. He had perhaps five seconds to find cover, while his enemies were still off balance, reeling from the blast.

The bench was made of stone and wood, as good a shield as he would find within a hundred yards. He scrambled over it and dropped into a crouch behind, as bullets started flying from the skirmish line of rebels. Bolan didn't see the second missile strike, but the report was clearly audible. A shock wave rolled across the park, and somebody screamed in the distance, from the pain of burns or shrapnel wounds.

He risked a glance around the bench, in time to see a pair of rebels closing on him, firing on the run. A rapid one-two punch from the Beretta in his right hand dropped one of the runners sprawling on his face, the other veering off from Bolan's line of fire. He ducked back as a stream of automatic fire chewed up the front side of the bench, scarring painted wood, chipping stone.

There was one down that he was sure of, and it stood to reason that at least a couple more had gone up when the cars exploded. He would have to hope so, anyway. Aristo had arrived with ten guns to support him, maybe others waiting in the wings, and in his present circumstances, Bolan doubted whether he could take them all before they flanked him, cut him off and got a clean shot at him from behind.

Which left some of the dirty work to the men of Phoenix Force.

He heard an AK-47 stutter to his right, McCarter switching from the RPG to the assault piece, laying down a screen of cover fire. A second rifle opened up, away to Bolan's left, which told him Katz was on the job.

They had triangulation now, a cross fire that would keep the rebels hopping. Bolan's enemies had lost their wheels and they were stranded, while converging streams of fire cut through their ranks.

But they weren't done yet by any means.

He heard Aristo's men returning fire in all directions, SMGs and scatterguns unloading at elusive targets. Bolan rose from cover, looking for the rebel leader, but he spotted something else instead. Off to his left, two men in khaki park-employee uniforms were removing automatic rifles from a plastic trash bag. To Bolan's right, a ''jogger'' had produced a stubby machine pistol from beneath his sweatshirt, squeezing off a burst toward McCarter's position.

A double trap, then. It could cut both ways.

He caught a quick glimpse of Aristo, breaking for the nearest trees, but Katz was off in that direction, blocking the escape route. Bolan was about to try a shot when one of Aristo's soldiers popped up in his line of fire. He squeezed off anyway, a parabellum mangler ripping through the gunner's chest to slam him on his back. A heartbeat later someone on his left cut loose with automatic fire and drove him under cover, angry hornets swarming in the air around his head.

Close calls.

He couldn't let the battle turn into a standoff, when police were almost certainly en route by now. A few more minutes and they would be out of time.

He came up firing, dropped another rebel in his tracks and broke from cover in a headlong dash. Aristo was already halfway to the street and putting more ground between them all the time. Eighty yards separated the two men, and the way was far from clear.

No matter.

He was on the blood scent now, and he wouldn't break off the hunt until one of them was dead.

KATZ HAD HIDDEN in the men's room, seated on a toilet with his feet up, braced against the door that gave his stall a modicum of privacy. He came out only when the place was clear, two minutes short of Bolan's scheduled rendezvous with Aristo. There would be no explaining his Kalashnikov if anyone walked in on him from that point forward. He would have to knock the man out and dump him in a toilet stall while he went about his business.

Killing strangers.

As it happened, no one wandered in to take a bladder break before the two cars came in view, pulled up and stopped. He watched Aristo's soldiers take up their positions, hung back in the shadows of the men's room entrance, picking out his targets, when a movement at the far left of his vision drew his eyes in that direction.

Park attendants were picking trash off the ground with little spears. They put the garbage they collected in one sack, a second dragging heavy in the left hand of the man who held it. Neither one of them was concentrating on his job, but rather staring toward the bench where Bolan sat.

It all fell into place at once—the racket of McCarter's RPG round slamming home into the lead car, screams and angry curses, gunshots ringing through the park. Katz saw the two "attendants" drop their spears and one half-empty bag. They removed automatic weapons from the other, swinging them around to cover Bolan as he made a frantic dive behind the bench.

Katz knew what he had to do. He swung up his AK-47, his index finger squeezing the trigger as he found his targets, hosing them from right to left and back again. The rifle bucked against his shoulder, spewing empty brass from the ejection port, the muzzle working hard to climb while the Phoenix Force commander held it down.

The nearest of his targets stumbled, lost his weapon, tried to catch himself with outflung hands, but there was no hope for him, with the dark blood spouting from his neck and chest. He hit the grass facedown and lay there, while his partner tried to duck away.

Too late.

The bullets found him, tore open his rib cage with the surgical precision of a meat ax, spinning him and dropping him ten feet behind his comrade.

Done.

But there were still nearly a dozen soldiers milling on the grass, Aristo one of them, directing his men as best he could. Katz swung his AK-47 in that direction, looking for a target, praying that he wouldn't be too late...for Bolan's sake, or for his own.

FIDEL ARISTO FELT as if his lungs were bursting. He hadn't run far, but panic set his pulse to racing, made him feel as if a fist were clenched around his heart.

It was a trap, despite his preparations, and his men were dying all around him. For the moment he could think of nothing but to save himself.

He didn't hear the shot, with so much shooting in the park behind him, but a bullet sizzled past his left ear, close enough to stir his hair. He veered off course, came close to falling as he spun to glance behind him, looking for the enemy.

A tall man with a pistol in each hand was gaining on him, closing fast. Aristo threw himself aside as both guns fired at once, the bullets cleaving air where he had stood a heartbeat earlier.

The lunge was all it took to spoil his balance, but he went down firing, squeezing off two quick rounds from his .45. He didn't strike his target, but the stranger had to dodge, dropped prone, and it was all the edge Aristo needed. In an instant he was on his feet and running like a track star, firing one more shot behind him as he sprinted toward the only cover close at hand.

The public washroom was a long brick building with a door at each end—one for women, and the other door for men. There would be a dividing wall, somewhere around the middle of the building, logic told him, but he didn't need a floor plan of the place to know it was his only chance. It was a fool's game, trying to outrun his enemies in daylight, bullets flying all around. If he could only stop the one who was pursuing him right now, Aristo thought, he still might have a chance to slip away before police arrived.

He was almost to the rest room when a stocky, gray-haired man stepped into view, emerging from the shadows there. Aristo was about to shout a warning when he saw the AK-47 in the stranger's hands and knew that he had lost all hope.

With nothing left to lose, Aristo charged. He still had five rounds in the .45, and he used four of them, saw his opponent staggered by a square hit to the chest before a burst of rifle bullets cut his legs from under him. Aristo fell across the AK-47's line of fire, no matter that the gunman might be dying even now. His world exploded in a flare of blinding light, and he was gone.

THE SIGHT of Katzenelenbogen going down gave Bolan extra speed. He cleared Aristo's crumpled body with a loping stride and reached his Phoenix Force comrade just as Katz slumped back into a seated posture, with his back against the wall. There was a pained look on the gruff Israeli's face, but no blood showing through his shirt.

Not yet.

"Kevlar," Katz told him, grinning as Bolan started ripping at his shirt. A shiny copper-jacketed projectile had indeed been stopped, some millimeters short of penetration, slightly to the left of Katzenelenbogen's heart.

"Are you all right?"

"Ribs hurt like hell," Katz told him with a grimace. "Something cracked, I wouldn't be surprised."

"Good thinking, with the vest. You got Aristo, too."

"Damn right."

"Can you stand?"

"I'm fine."

Katz struggled to his feet and followed Bolan back in the direction of the battlefield. They heard a siren wailing in the distance, clearly audible now that the gunfire had begun to sputter out.

Bolan counted two guerrillas on their feet, one of them staggering and clutching at his side as they retreated, making for the street. He palmed the little two-way radio and thumbed the switch to reach McCarter.

"Pulling back," he said. "Confirm."

"I hear you," the former SAS commando replied, "loud and clear."

"Let's go."

Katz shrugged his helping hand aside and said, "I'm not done yet. The day I can't walk to the car is the day I'll buy a one-way ticket home."

Aristo's death wouldn't eliminate the rebel threat on Mindanao, or elsewhere in the Philippines, but it would slow the left-wing army a little while new leaders were selected. Bolan didn't need a lot of time to wrap his mission in the islands, if he did it right. For now he was content to know that they had struck another blow against the Red Chinese—and, by extension, done more damage to the 14K.

His team was still intact, if somewhat battered from prolonged exposure to the enemy, and they had served him well so far. If Bolan squinted, he imagined he could see a faint light at the tunnel's end.

A red light.

It reminded him of fire and blood.

12

Manila

Hwak Tan thought it would be a good time for a short vacation, a reprieve of sorts. His major businesses were shut down in Manila, and they would stay that way until his enemies got tired of stalking him and went in search of other prey. The city wouldn't miss him for a time, and he could definitely use a break from all the pressure he had felt the past two days.

It wasn't manly, running from a problem in this fashion, but Tan wouldn't let his enemies dictate the way he lived his life. If he allowed himself to be a prisoner, trapped in Manila by the fear of men he didn't know, had never seen, there would be equal cowardice involved. By leaving he could demonstrate his personal contempt for those who tried to frighten him, defeat them by depriving them of targets, while his soldiers kept on scouring the streets.

Or so he told himself.

Tan called out for his houseman, nodded toward the two bags he had packed and watched the young man carry them away. The limousine was waiting for him just outside. A second car filled with gunmen would serve as an escort to the airport.

He was ready. There was nothing else to do that couldn't wait for his return, or else be taken care of by a simple order via telephone. His second-in-command could watch the city for him.

Tan would be traveling by charter jet to Taipei, and while he wouldn't have to pass through any checkpoints at the airport prior to his departure, weapons were forbidden on arrival in Taiwan. It made no difference, though, once Tan was in the air. His troubles would be far behind him in another hour, and he could show his enemies the scorn that they deserved.

He walked out to the car, and one of the soldiers opened the back door for him, while the others scrambled to their places. In another moment Hwak Tan was on his way.

He felt his troubles slipping from him, like a grim weight lifted off his shoulders. He sat back, relaxing in his seat, and started looking forward to a brand-new day.

THE BANDAGE GIRDLING Katzenelenbogen's chest was itching fiercely, and his cracked ribs throbbed, causing him to grit his teeth each time movement brought a sharper pain to life. He wore the Kevlar vest over his bandages, and that was even more uncomfortable in the muggy heat. Katz was convinced that he would break out in a nasty rash from neck to waist before the day was done.

Of course, he was extremely fortunate to be alive and itching, throbbing, aching—anything at all. Without the vest, Aristo would have killed him in Davao, and he wouldn't be standing in a dank Manila stairwell, waiting for the signal that McCarter was in place, prepared to make their move against Wong Kam.

Some luck, he thought, and instantly regretted it. A part of him still clung reluctantly to childhood teachings that a morbid thought meant tempting God to make your fears come true.

The jacket Katzenelenbogen wore had been necessary to conceal his submachine gun when he left the car outside and entered the apartment building. He went directly to the service stairs, avoiding contact with a Filipino janitor who had been sweeping up the lobby. Katz didn't expect the sweeper to come looking for him, but he was prepared for anything. The blackjack in his pocket should be adequate to keep the young man quiet for a while.

The two-way radio attached to Katzenelenbogen's belt wasn't much larger than a pack of cigarettes. It whispered to him now, the volume turned low to prevent McCarter's voice from echoing inside the stairwell.

"I'm inside."

Katz thumbed the button twice in answer, no response in words expected. He began to mount the stairs, six flights remaining before he reached the penthouse level where their target made his home. McCarter would be riding in the service elevator, timing his arrival so that he and Katz would reach the seventh floor together.

The Uzi had a bulky 12-inch silencer attached. He had considered ditching it, but finally decided he was better safe than sorry. Any edge they could attain against their enemies would help them through the early stages of the probe and put them closer to Wong Kam.

The word from Bolan's native contact was that Hwak Tan had detailed soldiers to protect his ChiCom ally, but they didn't know how many or how well they would be armed. All things considered, Katz was ready for the worst and hoping for the best.

His ribs were aching by the time he reached the final landing. He paused to catch his breath and listened at the access door before he made his move. Nothing.

He checked his watch and saw that it was time. If McCarter was late, Katz would know it soon enough.

The knob turned easily at Katzenelenbogen's touch, his claw firm on the brass, his good hand wrapped around the Uzi's pistol grip. He shouldered through as if he owned the place, glanced left along a stretch of empty hallway ending at a blank brick wall, then turned back to his right and let the door swing shut.

Four Chinese were staring at him, startled into immobility. Katz took advantage of the lull and raised his SMG, no hesitation in him as he braced the weapon's heavy muzzle with his claw and held down the trigger.

He swept the line from left to right and dropped two before the others hauled out their weapons and scattered, starting to return his fire. A bullet whispered past his ear and sweat broke out on his face as he dropped prone, ribs screaming at him from his impact with the floor.

Downrange, behind the gunners, he saw two doors open and men spill into the hallway.

And Katz knew that he was trapped.

THE LIMOUSINE and tail car were a quarter mile ahead of Bolan when he joined the convoy, driving south and picking up his speed to stay in touch. He hadn't jumped them as they left Tan's house because he hoped to find a better killing ground, away from innocent civilians and their vehicles. The run south to the airport offered possibilities, but he would have to make a judgment call when it was time.

Whatever happened, he didn't intend to let the red pole slip away.

They drove out Roxas Boulevard and caught the highway, heading south from town. The traffic thinned a bit once they had left Manila proper, and he started looking for a place to make his move. The tail car would be first, since it could block his access to the limousine, and only when the flankers were disposed of would he think about what kind of armor and defenses Tan might have incorporated into his crew wagon.

Bolan stood on the accelerator, gaining ground. They had a mile-long stretch of open highway, with no one else in a position to be harmed as he closed in on Tan and company. The left- and right-front windows of his rental car were down, the wind whipping at him in a rush as he accelerated toward his target.

Closing.

The Executioner kept his left hand on the wheel and reached out with his right to lift an MP-5 K submachine gun from the empty shotgun seat beside him. It was loaded with thirty armor-piercing rounds, the fire selector set for 3-round bursts. Anticipating trouble with his adversaries in a running fight, the Executioner had come prepared.

Somebody in the tail car had to have seen him coming. Two heads turned to watch him through the broad back window of the target vehicle, Chinese faces staring back at Bolan, frowning as they tried to figure out if he was trouble or a harebrained traveler running late for his flight. It almost seemed that they relaxed when Bolan started signaling to pass them on the left, and both grim faces vanished as he changed lanes, swinging around the car in front of him.

They weren't quite ready to dismiss him, though. He saw the driver checking him in the left-hand mirror, and another face was in the back seat window as he gunned it, drawing up beside the tail car. When he raised the MP-5 K into view, the driver saw it coming and swerved toward Bolan in a bid to spoil his aim. He fired a burst regardless and watched holes blossom on the door behind the driver's seat.

The nearest window powered down, and Bolan saw the muzzle of a gun emerging, swinging into target acquisition on his face. He tapped the brake and let the tail car pull ahead of him, the first rounds from his adversary wasted, flying high and wide across the hood of the rental car.

Bolan had to wrap this up without inordinate delay, or Tan would make tracks in the limo, lose him while the soldiers sacrificed themselves to slow him. That was the purpose of the tail car, after all—to fight a rearguard action while their master got away.

Not this time, though. The Executioner wasn't prepared to see the big fish wriggle through his net while he got stuck with the sardines.

He swerved around the back end of the tail car, coming up along the shoulder of the road. It was a risky move, but it would take the driver by surprise. If he was quick enough, maybe he could pull it off.

Still driving with his left hand, Bolan poked the MP-5 K submachine gun out his window, close enough that sighting was superfluous. He saw two faces turned in his direction, flushed with anger or excitement now, one of them shouting orders the Executioner couldn't hear.

He stroked the subgun's trigger twice, sending six rounds smashing through the safety glass, through flesh and bone. His third burst found the driver, striking from his blind side, slamming him against the wheel as blood and brains were spattered on the inside of the windshield.

Bolan tapped the brake again, drew back and watched the tail car swerving, left to right across the highway, finally spilling off the edge on one side, grass and gravel spewing from beneath its tires. It didn't roll, but Bolan wasn't worried. Even with a man or two still living in the chase car, it would take some time for them to drag a dead man from the driver's seat, restart the flooded engine and give chase. There was at least a fifty-fifty chance they wouldn't even try.

And in the meantime he was closing on Hwak Tan. The big fish was within his reach now, and the Executioner had no intention of losing him.

WONG KAM WAS in the bathroom when the shooting started. He hadn't been well the past twelve hours, suffering from a weakness in his bowels that made him both angry and embarrassed. He told himself that it was unrelated to the strain of recent events, but something in Kam's mind kept nagging at him, calling him a liar.

The first two pistol shots were muffled, intervening walls absorbing sound, but they were loud enough to startle Kam, bring him cursing to his feet to grapple with his stubborn trousers. He walked into his bedroom as three of Tan's soldiers burst into the room, wild-eyed, weapons in their hands.

"What is it?" Kam demanded.

"We don't know," one of them replied.

"Don't know? *Don't know!* Find out, you idiots! Why are you standing here, when there are enemies outside?"

"We were instructed—"

"To protect me," Kam interrupted him. "How better to perform that duty than by going out to kill my enemies? Now *move!*"

The Triad soldiers did as they were told. Kam heard them muttering to one another as they crossed the living room. They hesitated at the door, debating tactics, but their only real choice was to go or stay, and they had been commanded to engage the enemy. He heard the front door open, gunfire louder with that barrier removed, until it closed again.

Tan had sent eight soldiers to protect him from the unknown enemy. It came down to a kind of house arrest, but Kam hadn't complained. The obvious alternative held no appeal.

But now...

Kam crossed the bedroom to the nightstand. In the top drawer was a loaded 9 mm Makarov pistol. The weapon had a live round in the chamber, with the hammer down. Kam simply had to cock it with his thumb, and he was ready.

There was no time to pack, as if he could get past his adversaries carrying a suitcase. Getting past them, period, would be a challenge. Tan's soldiers might get lucky, but he thought about the others who had died so far and knew he didn't want to trust the odds.

That was the problem with a penthouse in a public building: no escape hatch to the world outside. Kam's only exit was the front door, where a battle raged between his enemies and eight men pledged to guard him with their lives.

Kam thought of calling the police and instantly dismissed the notion. It would be useless; his neighbors had to have called already. Squad cars would be racing toward the scene, their high-pitched sirens wailing through the streets. All Kam had to do was hold his ground and wait for reinforcements to arrive.

Kam did what he could under the circumstances. Crossing to the bedroom door, he closed and locked it, then went to sit on his bed, the pistol at his side.

To wait for life or death.

THE SEVENTH FLOOR was chaos when McCarter stepped out of the service elevator. He had heard the sounds of gunfire from the floor below, albeit muffled and distorted. Now he found himself smack in the middle of a shooting gallery, with Katz at the far end of the corridor and half a dozen gunmen in between, all dodging, pumping lead at Katz, while trying to protect themselves. A couple who had failed in that regard were stretched out on the carpet, as still as death.

McCarter's MP-5 SD-3 submachine gun had a built-on silencer, and while it seemed superfluous in the prevailing racket of the corridor, he took advantage of it, striking from the blind side of his enemies with muffled rounds that ripped into their backs. There was no chivalry in mortal combat, and McCarter put two of them down before the others noticed what was happening, the nearest of them pivoting to bring him under fire.

The Briton shot his adversary in the chest and saw him slump against the wall, bright streaks of crimson painted on the wallpaper as he went down. That still left three, and

Katz dropped one of them before McCarter had a chance to frame another target in his sights.

The last two Chinese were cut off, and they knew it, dodging twin streams of converging fire and shooting back with pistols. When they bolted, both of them at once, one broke toward the door of Kam's penthouse suite, the other charging toward the elevator—and McCarter.

It wasn't the smartest move he could have made. The Briton met him with a rising burst that yanked the soldier off his feet and slammed him over on his backside, wriggling on the floor as life pumped out through round holes in his chest. Katz had the other one, meanwhile, a long burst from the Uzi driving him headfirst into the door with force enough to clear the threshold.

Scrambling to his feet, McCarter fed his SMG with a replacement magazine and saw Katz reloading as he moved toward the open penthouse door. The first man through was risking everything, but there was no time to debate the call.

McCarter took the lead, a headlong rush that brought him up behind a sofa, swiveling to check the living room and the adjacent kitchen, tracking with his SMG.

There were no signs of life, but he didn't believe eight guards would have been detailed to protect an empty flat. That left the bedrooms, down a hallway to his left, and he was moving in that direction when Katz came up on his heels. McCarter heard him breathing hard, glanced back and noted that a kind of pallor seemed to underlay the tough Israeli's baked-in tan.

"Are you all right?"

"I'm fine," Katz snapped. "Let's do it."

"Right."

Three doors lined the hallway: left, right and straight ahead. Katz took the left and found the bathroom empty, while McCarter checked a vacant bedroom on the right.

And that left one.

"On three?"

Katz nodded, stepping to one side and leveling his Uzi from the hip. McCarter took the other wall and held his SMG rock-steady in his hands, starting to count.

On "three," both men unloaded half a magazine into the door, some thirty rounds exploding through the flimsy wooden panel. Instantly, with echoes of the gunfire ringing in his ears, McCarter vaulted forward, slammed a flying kick into the riddled door and plunged through in a diving shoulder roll, with Katz behind him, bringing up the rear.

The first two pistol shots were high and wide, both wasted, and McCarter had his target fixed before Kam could fire again. The ChiCom diplomat was on his knees behind a king-size bed, the pistol held in front of him in a stiff two-handed grip.

The Briton let loose with his subgun as Kam tried to turn and bring him under fire, a 3-round burst enough to punch the human target over on his back. A last round from Kam's pistol drilled the ceiling. Edging cautiously around the bed, McCarter found the man stretched out on the floor, a raw hole in his forehead and another in the right side of his throat, below the jawline.

Done.

Katz was beside McCarter as the commando scrambled to his feet. "We should be going," the Israeli said.

"Sounds right."

They put that place of death behind them, rode the service elevator down to save time and heard the sirens drawing closer as they stepped into an alley at the rear of the apartment building. The rental car was parked a block away, an easy walk if no one tried to intercept them.

Glancing at Katz again, McCarter saw his friend was sweating, felt a question churning in his mind, but kept it to himself.

There would be time enough for questions when the job was done.

IT WAS A TRICK, reloading while he held the rental steady, pushing eighty miles an hour, but Bolan got it done. The limousine was fifty yards ahead of him, then forty, thirty, running for it, but hampered by the very size and weight that made it so attractive to a man of means.

He ran up on the vehicle's tail, hung close and steady, waiting for his chance. The limo driver tried to make it harder for him, weaving back and forth across the road, fishtailing. It made passing difficult, but at the same time it prevented Bolan's enemies from firing on him, since he couldn't pull abreast, and hanging out a window to fire backward would have left them too exposed.

He took the MP-5 K in his left hand and held it out the window, with his wrist braced on the mirror. When the limo again started drifting to its left, he swung the rental to his right, lined up a quick bead on the broad back window of Tan's vehicle and squeezed off a burst of six or seven rounds.

He got immediate results.

The limo swerved more violently, the wheelman almost losing it. The safety glass imploded, raining shiny pebbles on the limo's occupants, Tan among them. Bolan fired another burst and saw two rounds strike the trunk lid, others whipping through the open window, taking out a portion of the windshield as they passed completely through the passenger compartment.

Bolan took advantage of the big car's weaving course to run up on the driver's side, the MP-5 K in his right hand now, and aimed across the empty seat beside him. He was ready when a tinted window started gliding down into its slot, a big fistful of hardware poking out. He held down the submachine gun's trigger and ripped that arm to bloody tatters, kept on firing as he passed the limousine, dark window glass exploding. Someone screamed, audible above the sounds of gunfire, engine noise and screeching tires.

He saw the limo veer off course and shoot across the gravel shoulder of the highway, then down a steep embankment. It rolled over several times, stopping finally against a barbed-wire fence. Bolan braked and put the rental in reverse. He parked and left the engine running, taking the MP-5 K and a heavy gym bag with him as he walked back to the point where tire tracks marked the limo's steep descent.

He stood above the capsized vehicle and watched a shadow-figure grappling with a door behind the driver's, straining hard to open it. The guy was halfway out when Bolan shot him in the chest and dumped him back inside the car. A frightened voice called out from somewhere in the limousine, and the warrior sent another burst downrange to pin the stunned survivors where they were.

He set the gym bag at his feet, unzipped it, reached inside and lifted out a thermite canister. He yanked the pin, lined up the pitch and lobbed it overhand. The fat grenade dropped through a shattered window of Tan's limousine, producing yet another startled cry before it detonated seconds later.

Bolan stood and watched the limo burning for a moment, confident that no one could survive in that inferno. He was halfway to his vehicle when the gas tank blew and settled any doubts that might have lingered in his mind.

Another red pole up in smoke.

He turned the car around and started back in the direction of Manila. It was time to meet his Phoenix Force comrades and prepare to catch another flight.

The climax of their mission was approaching.

They were heading off to face the Dragon in his lair.

13

Hong Kong

There was no question why they named it Fragrant Harbor, Katz decided, but the man or men responsible had certainly possessed a sense of humor. It wasn't so much a fragrance, the Israeli reckoned, as it was a stench—a mix of dead fish, diesel fumes and the aroma of too many people crowded into too little space. Six million people thronged the island, all but 200,000 of them Chinese, which translated into thousands of people for each square kilometer of land. Small wonder, then, that everything about the island struck a visitor as crowded, rushed, a sense of urgency exacerbated by reversion to mainland control that would take place within a year.

The waterfront was where it all hit home. Junks and sampans crowded into the marina, each with its own family living in close quarters—eating, sleeping, breeding on the water—while vast cargo ships, cruise liners and warships disgorged a nonstop flow of money and humanity.

Katz motored past the warehouse once, to check for guards outside, then doubled back to find a parking place. The night was warm, and he was driving with his window down despite the smell. Since there was no escaping it this close to the water, he had opted for total immersion, compelling himself to adapt.

The duffel bag beside him weighed forty pounds and clanked when Katzenelenbogen placed it on the empty shotgun seat. He ran the zipper down and reached inside, took out the MP-5 K submachine gun, several extra magazines and two thermite canisters. When Katz had everything he needed from the bag, he zipped it again, returned it to the floor beneath the dash and started suiting up for war.

The swivel rig beneath his sport coat was attached to Katz's shoulder holster, his Browning automatic underneath his right arm, while the SMG would hang below his left. Spare magazines went in his pockets, and the thermite bombs clipped onto the Israeli's belt. Emerging from the car, he spent a moment double-checking the belt and shoulder harness. His cracked ribs pained him, making him adjust the harness, then he locked the car and started back in the direction of his target.

They were at last in the final stretch, Katz thought. The warehouse was a property of Edward Wong, the hill chief of the 14K. The boss of bosses, as it were. They had been some time getting here, a long road fraught with peril, and he hoped it would be worth the wait.

Three late-model cars were parked against the loading dock, all in the upper price range. Katz had company, and that was fine. It seemed a shame to come this far and raid an empty storage depot, when he could get right to business, tangling with the hill chief's soldiers.

He had to watch his step. It was important that he not be overconfident, not let himself be drawn into a fatal error for ego's sake. The rest of it had all been a rehearsal for the Hong Kong blitz, where every move was critical.

Like now.

He shunned the loading dock, where lights were burning overhead, and walked around the east side of the warehouse, where he found a door that opened at his touch. Could that be right?

Katz paused and sniffed the air, as if to smell a trap, but there was nothing. Only fish and diesel fumes.

He brought the MP-5 K from under cover, thumbed off the safety and held it ready as he stepped across the threshold into darkness.

BOLAN LEFT HIS RENTAL in the underground garage and rode the elevator up eleven floors to Huang-se Enterprises. These were strictly corporate offices, no merchandise on hand, and that was fine. The company was one of Edward Wong's, created by the Triad hill chief and controlled through a minimaze of paper companies that minimized tax liability while leaving Wong in ready contact with the cash.

It wouldn't be a body blow, per se, but Huang-se Enterprises represented one step closer to respectability, a goal most wealthy gangsters staked out for themselves, sometime in middle age. A strike against Huang-se would be a shot to Wong's ego and his wallet, all at once—a nasty one-two punch that had to hurt, even if it didn't cause permanent damage.

He caught a break, considering the hour, and had the elevator to himself. Most times, at rush hours and lunchtime, it would be jammed full like a sardine can, with a designated "pusher" standing by to make sure no one had an inch of extra breathing room.

The Hong Kong way.

Eleven came, and Bolan stepped out into a capacious hallway, spotted numbers mounted on the wall directly opposite, with arrows, and proceeded to his left. Most of the offices he passed were closed now, locked up for the night, their lights switched off, but Wong's employees were well-known for working overtime. It hardly mattered in the long run whether anyone was home or not, but he acknowledged to himself that it would help to have somebody spread the word, tell Wong exactly what had happened and relay a brief description of the enemy.

The tall glass doors were open, and he shouldered through, confronted by a young Chinese receptionist who met him with a cheery smile, as if he were the first arrival of the day instead of someone straggling in near closing time. Her English was the next best thing to flawless.

"May I help you, sir?"

"I need to see the manager," Bolan said.

"May I say who's calling?"

"He wouldn't recognize my name," Bolan replied, showing her the Uzi that he carried underneath his jacket, "but I think he'll see me, anyway."

She lost her smile, considered screaming, then thought better of it. "This way," she said, and rose on shaky legs to lead him down a narrow corridor, past watercooler, rest rooms and a row of doors on either side that had been marked with names in English and Chinese. He made a mental note that three of those small offices were occupied, which put men at his back when he was ready to withdraw.

Still hooked on the proprieties, his escort knocked and waited at the last door on their left. A high-pitched, sexless voice gave her permission to proceed, and Bolan followed her into the inner sanctum. Hunched behind a spacious, cluttered desk, a chunky man who had to be pushing fifty glanced up from his paperwork, saw Bolan with the Uzi in his hand and dropped his slim gold-plated pen.

"There must be some mistake," he said.

"You made it when you went to work for Edward Wong," the Executioner replied.

"I don't know—"

Bolan raked the wall above his head with half a dozen parabellum rounds. The woman screamed, his target ducked out of sight, and the warrior was already half turned toward the open doorway when the other three men arrived, all gaping at the damage, cringing from the weapon they found pointed at their faces. All were younger than their boss, all smartly dressed, with hair just so.

"You must be wondering why I called you here, today," the Executioner said, unable to resist a smile. "I'm after Wong, the 14K, whatever he lays hands on. Get it? You're not soldiers, and I'd just as soon not kill you, but the choice is yours. I'm taking out the files, all the financial records. You can either leave or hang around and watch it all go up in smoke. What will it be?"

The five captives hesitated, glancing back and forth at one another, trying to decide if he was serious. Thirty seconds passed before the first one bolted, and when Bolan didn't gun him down, the others followed in a rush. He caught the manager by one plump arm and held him back a moment, leaning in so that their noses almost touched, the Uzi wedged beneath his captive's chin.

"Tell Wong that this is only the beginning. He's been waiting for me, since I started out in San Francisco. Now I'm here. Can you remember that?"

The middle-aged man blinked twice and gave a jerky nod. His voice had dried up on him somehow, but it was enough to satisfy the Executioner. He loosened his grip and watched the last rat scuttle off the sinking ship.

The file cabinets were unlocked for easy access during business hours, and he placed a slim incendiary stick in each middle drawer to guarantee results. He set another fire stick on the manager's desk, and one each for the lesser offices where flunkies spent their daylight hours tracking merchandise or juggling balance sheets. He wedged the last incendiary under the receptionist's computer, almost as an afterthought.

And he was out of there before the first one sizzled into glaring, white-hot life, already riding down to the garage. A janitor got in on six, stepped off on three, and Bolan was alone once more. The underground garage was bright with overhead fluorescent lights, but cooler than the city streets outside. He fine-tuned the rental's air conditioner and left the windows shut as he drove up the ramp.

Round one, but he wasn't about to score a knockout yet. He still had work to do in Hong Kong, and it would be getting harder, bloodier, as Bolan went along.

You didn't take out a Dragon by yanking on its tail, but it was a beginning. Later, when the time was right, then he would cut off the monster's head.

Assuming he was still alive.

KATZ FOUND HIS TARGETS playing dominoes for money, four men hunched around a table, their heads bowed underneath a cloud of rank tobacco smoke. He could have killed them where they sat, the MP-5 K steady in his hand, but he cleared his throat and called to them instead.

"Game's over!"

Startled faces turned in his direction, soldiers frozen in a stark tableau, uncertain whether they should try to reach their guns or simply wait and find out what the crazy white man wanted. Considering the state of education in Hong Kong, Katz guessed that one of them, at least, should be an English speaker who could translate for the rest if they weren't bilingual.

"On your feet!" he snapped.

The four men hesitated briefly, then obeyed without a word between them.

"Put your hands up. Up, I said!"

They reluctantly did as they were told, like extras in a holdup scene from some old Western movie. Katz approached them, doing rapid calculations in his head. Three cars outside, four players at the table. If a couple of them shared a ride...

The sound of rushing footsteps came from Katzenelenbøgen's left flank, and he turned swiftly to confront the fifth man, rushing at him with distorted features, brandishing a knife and winding up to cut loose with a martial artist's scream.

Katz shot him in the chest, a 3-round burst that snatched him off his feet and dumped him over backward, shoulders hitting the concrete floor before his heels and buttocks got there. There was a metallic clatter as he lost the knife and it went skimming off across the floor.

More scuffling, and Katz turned to find the others scattering like roaches in a kitchen, startled by a sudden show of light. They broke in all directions, one quick-thinking as he tipped over the table, spilling dominoes, and dropped behind it. That was flimsy cover, but it gave him time to draw his pistol while the other three were running for their lives.

Katz stitched a line of holes across the tabletop to take him out or pin him down, then spun to catch the nearest runner in midstride, already closing on the cover of some wooden crates on the Israeli's right. A swarm of parabellum manglers caught the Triad hardman halfway there and rolled him up like someone's rag doll, tumbling in a boneless sprawl that left him stretched out on his back, eyes open, staring at the vaulted ceiling as they glazed.

The Phoenix Force commander swung around to catch another runner, this one pounding arrow-straight along an aisle between two rows of cardboard cartons large enough to hold refrigerators. Half a dozen bullets stitched a ragged line of holes along the target's spine and pitched him forward, sliding on his face across the shiny concrete floor.

One runner remained, and Katz was swiveling to take him when a shape sprang up behind the capsized table, leveling an automatic in both hands. He saw the muzzle-flash and felt something like a hammer strike his solar plexus. Katz went down hard, his impact with the cold concrete collaborating with the stomach punch to empty out his lungs. The vest had saved him from a gut shot, but he couldn't breathe, not yet. He felt like he was drowning, and his fingers loosened on the submachine gun, even as his brain cried out for them to hang on tight.

A shadow loomed above him, pistol pointed at his head, the round face scowling. The man expected blood and bent down to examine Katz, quick fingers ripping at the tough Israeli's shirt to find out why he wasn't dead. The Phoenix Force commander was staring at his adversary when the Triad gunner swung his pistol in a looping arc, directly at his captive's skull.

The lights went out.

THE BARRETT FIFTY is a monster, chambered for the Browning .50-caliber machine-gun cartridge, with a 10-round magazine. Its thirty-six-inch barrel and internal recoil mechanism help reduce the weapon's kick to something on the order of a 12-gauge shotgun firing magnum loads, but there is no relief for flesh and bone on the receiving end. Specifically designed for stopping vehicles and stalking barricaded snipers in an urban combat zone, the rifle has been marketed to wealthy sportsmen as the ultimate big-game piece. All you need to drop that elephant or grizzly with the Barrett is $3,000 cash, the necessary permits and a marksman's skill.

McCarter wedged the Barrett's stock against his shoulder, peering through the telescopic sight. In theory, he could drop a man-size target at three thousand feet, but he wasn't about to try it. Stretched out on the flat roof of a semitrailer, two hundred yards from Michael Hoy's front door, a half mile east of Garden Road, he meant to shake up the natives a little, let them feel the heat and rob the 14K of its most infamous enforcer in Hong Kong.

He waited, ticking off the moments, and felt a warm surge of relief when Hoy and two young bodyguards emerged from the apartment building, moving swiftly toward the car that waited for them. The driver stepped out to walk around and get the door for his employer.

Nice and tidy.

There was no such thing as hollowpoints in .50-caliber, so McCarter had packed the Barrett's magazine with armor-piercing rounds. If it was good enough for quarter-inch steel plate, it ought to do the trick on Chevalier, flesh and bone. He fixed the cross hairs on his target's face, breathed deeply, held it and tightened his index finger on the rifle's trigger.

Boom!

No way to silence that report. Downrange, Hoy's skull exploded into crimson mist. The headless body toppled to the ground like a puppet with its strings cut.

And the bodyguards went wild.

It had been bad enough, McCarter told himself, when Hoy's blood spattered their faces, but the worst part had to be realizing they were next. He swung the Barrett's muzzle several inches to the left and fired another shot before the echo of the first one died away, one of the Triad soldiers spinning like a top, blood spraying from his mutilated chest.

And that left two.

The driver was circling around the car for some reason, instead of simply diving through the open door in back. More proof that force of habit could be fatal, as McCarter tracked him with the Barrett. His third shot slammed the runner hard against his vehicle, a giant drop-kicking a scarecrow, and the young man's arm was ripped clear of its socket, dangling by mere shreds of flesh and fabric as he fell.

The sole survivor was already halfway back to the apartment building and running for his life. McCarter fixed the cross hairs in the middle of his back and stroked the Barrett's trigger twice. It was a case of overkill, impact lifting his target clear of the pavement, slamming him facefirst through the glass doors of the lobby, dumping him inside.

McCarter took out his earplugs and started breaking down the field artillery. Dismantled, it would fit inside the thirty-eight-inch duffel bag that he had carried from his car. It was an awkward burden, even with the canvas shoulder strap, and the Briton endured rough thumps against his hip as he scrambled down the iron rungs of the ladder that had granted access to the semitrailer's roof.

There were no witnesses in sight, and he was safe inside his rental car before a doorman stepped across the threshold to survey the carnage on the sidewalk.

Time to go.

Hong Kong was heating up, and it wouldn't be long before the hill chief of the 14K began to smell the smoke.

GOOD NEWS WAS HARD to come by these days, but it seemed that Edward Wong had caught a break. It was the first time in three weeks that he hadn't been apprehensive when he telephoned the Dragon in Macau. And while it would be premature to say the tide had turned, he still felt optimistic. Cautiously so, but optimistic all the same.

He got one of the Dragon's flunkies, as usual, and waited while the underling went off to fetch his master. Moments later Cheung Kuo was on the line, a note of apprehension in his own voice that betrayed the strain he had been under since their scheme began to fall apart.

"You have some news?" the Dragon asked without preamble.

"Good news for a change," Wong replied. "We've caught one of the round-eyes."

"What? When did this happen? Where?"

"Within the hour," Wong replied. "Right here in Hong Kong."

"So they've found you, then."

"Was that in doubt?"

The Dragon gave no answer; none was necessary. "What do you intend to do?" he asked instead.

"I have the bait," Wong told him. "Logic dictates I should build a trap."

"It would be well, indeed, if this was all behind us."

"Only time was needed for our enemies to make a fatal error," Wong replied. "Now they have played into our hands."

"You will interrogate the prisoner?" Kuo asked.

"It is beginning as we speak."

"Keep me informed," the Dragon said.

"Of course."

The Dragon seldom said goodbye. It was a quirk of personality, perhaps, that he was prone to hang up when he felt a conversation was concluded, leaving Wong with nothing but a dial tone humming in his ear. This day the rudeness didn't irritate him, though.

He had a prize in hand, and if he dealt with it correctly, it could be enough to let him crush his enemies. That vengeance would be sweet, when he had suffered so much injury and personal humiliation during recent weeks. An extra bonus, separate from the destruction of the triggermen responsible for murdering so many of Wong's men, would be the information he extracted from the prisoner.

The Triad had long arms. They spanned the globe, and no one was beyond Wong's reach when he set out to punish persons who offended him. It mattered not if traitors and defectors from his family hid out in Beirut, Maracaibo or Johannesburg. Wong always paid his debts, and he expected nothing less from those who owed him blood for their transgressions.

Once he determined who had sent these men to vex him and disrupt his family, he would return the favor, even if he had to strike in Washington, D.C. No man defied the 14K and lived to boast about it. It had been several years since Wong reached out to kill a government official—and the victim in that case hadn't been an American—but it was all the same, in principle.

Before he could begin to make a list of targets, though, his men would have to wring some answers from the gunman they had captured. He would almost certainly resist at first, but there were ways of getting information from a man that no one could resist. Beyond a certain point, the drugs and suffering combined to overcome resistance from the strongest will and left a hollow shell behind.

Still, there would be time enough for this unlucky one to comprehend the moment of his death, which wouldn't be easy for him, either. If he thought interrogation was a trial, his execution would be even more excruciating.

Wong didn't intend to miss it. He could use some entertainment at the moment, something that would make him smile. What better than the death screams of an enemy to perk up his spirits?

The hill chief owed it to himself.

He wouldn't be denied.

THE WARRIORS MET at Statue Square in downtown Hong Kong.

Two of them.

"Where is he, dammit?" McCarter asked, talking to himself as much as to Bolan.

"Maybe he got hung up."

"He had the shortest list of anyone," the Briton said. "I think there's something wrong with him."

"Wrong, how?"

"I can't put my finger on it, really. First he talks about his age, then laughs it off. I watch him, and it seems like things are coming harder to him than they used to."

Bolan thought about it, frowning. Everybody aged, if they lived that long. Katz had at least a dozen years on Bolan, seldom showing it…but even once could get you killed.

It made unsettling food for thought, but they would have to talk about it later, when their mission was completed—assuming Katz turned up at all.

"Let's take a drive," Bolan suggested.

It was crazy, sitting still in public when they knew the 14K was looking for them—seeking someone they could blame for the attacks on Edward Wong and company. They killed an hour, driving aimlessly and doubling back to Statue Square every ten or fifteen minutes for another look around.

No sign of Katz.

"What's happened to him, then?" McCarter asked.

"I think," Bolan said, "that we'd better run a back-track on his target list and see what we can find."

14

Hong Kong's police department, although staffed primarily by native officers in uniform, remained a British institution to the core. Chinese held two-thirds of the detective posts, and they included a number of command-grade officers, but the decisions handed down from city hall on major issues came from Britons, who would control the colony for several months yet, until their lease expired in 1997 and the island passed to Chinese hands.

Detective Sergeant David Lau wasn't entirely sure that the change would be a bad thing. At one point in his life, he would have sworn it meant the end of civilized society in Hong Kong, a reversion to some stark political Dark Age of poverty, repression and an exodus of capital.

But there had been changes on the mainland, certainly, a strong trend toward the Western style of doing business—to the point, in fact, that China had become a major headache to America, producing bootleg films and music CDs by the ton. Besides, after nineteen years of working on the streets in Hong Kong, trying to clean up the mess that drugs, sex, greed and simple negligence left behind, Lau figured some kind of drastic change was in order.

The city no longer seemed so civilized to Lau. The normal cutthroat atmosphere had only been exacerbated as the clock ran down to 1997 and "the change." Already, certain businessmen were prepared to flee and take their op-

erations with them to Taiwan, the Philippines or the United
States. If Red control meant driving out the corporate
raiders, the narcotics dealers, the extortionists and loan
sharks, maybe it would all be for the best.

From what Lau picked up on the streets, though, members of the largest Triad in Hong Kong—the dreaded 14K—
had slacked off on their preparations for a move the past
twelve months or so. Lau's network of informants told him
little more than what his eyes could pick out as he made his
rounds. The troops of Edward Wong were digging in instead of bailing out, as if they knew a secret hidden from
the rest of Hong Kong's residents.

Lau had been working overtime, without success, to find
out what that secret was. This morning's order was unwel-
come, since it kept him from his work, but he wasn't in a
position to decline. When city hall instructed him to meet
with an American named Mike Belasko at a given time and
place, Lau could only rearrange his schedule and obey.

Lau didn't have a clue as to the subject of the meeting.
His immediate superior, Commander Winston Smythe, had
told him that it "might be something interesting" and let
it go at that. Lau hoped it wouldn't be another boring and
redundant lecture on the Triads by some G-man who was
earning college credit for an all-expenses-paid trip around
the world, imparting wisdom to benighted natives in the
name of Uncle Sam.

If nothing else, at least he might get breakfast out of it.
The meeting had been scheduled at a restaurant on Chater
Road near the courthouse. Lau knew the place but only
stopped in once or twice a year, when he had business to
discuss with prosecutors on a special case and he had failed
to catch them at the office.

Now a stranger. An American, no less. What could it
mean?

Lau found a parking space and locked his unmarked car.
Inside the restaurant, he asked for Mike Belasko, and the

hostess led him to a corner table, where a tall American sat drinking coffee, quietly appraising Lau with cool blue eyes.

The detective introduced himself and shook hands briefly, no commitment evident on either side. He took a seat, ordered an omelet and waited for the waitress to retreat before he spoke to the American.

"So, what's this all about?" he asked.

Bolan faced him squarely and replied, "I'm looking for a man to help me roast the 14K."

CONTACTING STONY MAN had been a last resort for Bolan. He had backtracked Katzenelenbogen's list of targets, found that none apparently had been disturbed. That told him the Israeli had been intercepted on—or prior to—his first attack in Hong Kong. Somehow Katz had landed in a mess that kept him from completing his assignments and regrouping back at Statue Square, as planned.

The only question now was whether he was still alive.

It made a difference with respect to Bolan's personal response. If Katz was dead, then there was nothing to be done for him, except to give their common enemy the scorched-earth special treatment. On the other hand, if he was still alive, then Bolan had to think about the possibility of liberating him, by any means available. Until he had some kind of information, one way or the other, any hasty moves could make things worse for Katz. For all they knew, he might be held at one of Wong's facilities marked for demolition. They would have to take it easy, relatively speaking, until they had some general idea of where he was, and whether he was still alive.

Which brought him back to Hal Brognola and the team at Stony Man. Through Brognola's connections to the British embassy and to the international police establishment, a link was made in Hong Kong. Bolan didn't know if it would help, but he could think of no one else more likely to have active eyes and ears inside the 14K.

Now, facing David Lau across the breakfast table, Bolan still had no idea if he was wasting precious time. It could go either way.

"What did you have in mind?" the detective asked.

Bolan knew that he would have to share a measure of the truth if he expected Lau to help—or even understand his needs. That didn't mean it was confession time, but they couldn't proceed without communication.

"I've been working on a covert operation against Edward Wong," he said.

"On British soil?"

"We made a stop in London earlier," Bolan replied. "Now we're here."

"Who's 'we'?" Lau asked.

"I'm not alone."

"That's not an answer."

"Put it this way," Bolan said. "We're on official business, but we're operating under rules of plausible deniability."

"You're CIA?"

"Not quite."

"All right, let's skip that for the moment. If it's so hush-hush, I don't see why we're talking. The Hong Kong police aren't on loan to agents from another country, most especially when their activities are likely to involve disruption of the public peace or violation of existing laws."

"I need your help," Bolan said, cutting to the chase.

"How's that?"

"One of my friends is missing. He went out last night to do a job and never made it back."

"A job involving members of the 14K?"

"That's right."

"Was it completed?"

"No."

Lau frowned. "Then it wouldn't have anything to do with the assassination of a man named Michael Hoy, who had his head blown off last night, along with several of his soldiers?''

"Definitely not."

"And if I asked if you had any notion of the trigger-man's identity?''

"I would deny it absolutely," Bolan said.

"Of course. And the fire last night at Huang-se Enterprises is a sheer coincidence, I suppose.''

"Could be."

"I've never liked coincidence," Lau stated. "I get suspicious."

"What I'm hoping," Bolan said, "is that you may have someone working with the 14K, or close enough to tell me if they have my man. I need to know if he's alive or dead.''

"And if I do, what then?"

"If he's alive, then I hope to get him back. I owe him that.''

"Are you prepared to deal with Edward Wong?" the sergeant asked.

"I've handled similar negotiations in the past."

"Successful?"

"Let's say I win more than I lose."

"If there's a kidnapping involved," Lau said, "then prosecution is appropriate. Conversely, if your man put Edward Wong in a position where he felt compelled to act in self-defense, *he* may see fit to file a charge.''

"I doubt that very much, and so do you."

"I have to look at all contingencies," Lau told him.

"Right now the only question that concerns me would be whether you can help. And if so, are you willing?''

"How much of this story did you tell to my superiors?" Lau asked.

"I've never spoken to them," Bolan said, deciding it was time to play his ace. "The contact came through Washington.''

"I see." Lau thought about that for a moment, taking in the implications. He was clearly apprehensive, even though he didn't seem prepared to challenge his superiors. At last he said, "There may be someone I can ask."

"And let me know as soon as possible?"

"How would I get in touch with you?"

"I'll check in at your office number," Bolan said. "How much time will you need?"

"To find my source and ask the question, possibly two hours. As to when I may receive an answer, if at all..."

He left it hanging, the uncertainty no more or less than Bolan had expected. They were gambling, plain and simple. Katz's life was riding on the line—if he was still alive at all—and it was no sure thing by any means.

"Whatever you can do," Bolan said, "I'll appreciate it."

"I had best get started then." Lau pushed back his plate, rising as he spoke. "Do you believe that what you're doing will impede the Triads in some way?"

"We live in hope," the Executioner replied.

"I wish you luck," the sergeant said. "Of course, if it should come to my attention that you've broken any laws in Hong Kong, I'll be forced to take another view."

"That's understood."

Lau checked his watch and said, "Call me at noon. I may have something for you, and if not..." He shrugged and turned away, walking out and disappearing into the street.

Four hours, give or take. It could turn out to be a lifetime, in the killing zone. The time wouldn't be wasted, though. They might be forced to wait for word from Lau's connections as to whether Katzenelenbogen was alive or dead, but there could be no doubt about the men responsible in either case.

Wong's troops had already experienced a taste of Bolan's wrath, but nothing like the full effect. They were about to get a preview, though, of what they could expect.

And old Hong Kong would never be the same.

KATZ KNEW THAT he was naked within seconds after waking. The cold concrete beneath him raised goose bumps on his skin, but it was not all bad. The chill helped counteract a bitter throbbing in his skull, almost suppressed the nausea that overwhelmed him for a moment, fading only by degrees.

As he reached up toward the round bump on his scalp, Katz found that they had also taken his prosthetic arm. The 14K were nothing, if not thorough.

Groaning like a wounded animal, he sat up, braced his back against a rough brick wall and had a look around the room that was his prison cell. There were no windows, nothing in the way of furniture. The single light bulb overhead was caged in metal; there was no switch in the room to turn it off. A plastic bucket, standing near the door, was clearly meant to be his chamber pot.

Katz thought back to the moment of his capture, felt humiliation vying for dominance with the pain inside his head. He had been careless—stupid, really—letting one of them sneak up on him. It had all caved in from there, and he was finished now. There could be no more generous interpretation of his circumstances.

Any way you sliced it, he was as good as dead.

The worst part was that he would be denied a chance to fight before they finished him. He still had elbows, fist and feet, of course, but it would be too much to hope for stupid negligence from his captors.

To Katz's way of thinking, he had sewn up that category all by himself.

The best thing he could do for Bolan and McCarter was to resist all efforts at interrogation. There was no doubt in his mind that someone would be dropping by to question him. They would have simply killed him, otherwise, and dumped his body in the harbor. He was alive because they needed him, and what else could he offer to the 14K but information on his comrades?

Katz would die before he let himself betray the others. That was carved in stone. But, at the same time, he was wise enough to know that no man could resist the latest methods of interrogation endlessly. If pain failed to produce a breakthrough, there were drugs to do the job, some of them absolutely irresistible.

Which meant that he would have to make the bastards kill him, somehow, stage an incident before they could begin to question him in earnest, force their hand, by one means or another.

Make them lose control.

He couldn't kill himself, but if he took his captors by surprise and pushed them far enough . . .

The thought of dying didn't frighten Katz. He had been flirting with the Reaper since he first put on a military uniform, had felt the cold breath on his neck a thousand times before, but it had always passed him by. The arm aside, he couldn't complain about a run of luck that had allowed him to survive this long, against all odds.

Few soldiers were permitted to select the place and hour of their deaths. That was a privilege most frequently reserved for suicides. Katz, for his part, would be choosing death as a strategic move, one final blow against his enemies.

He struggled to his feet as footsteps sounded in the corridor outside. A key turned in the lock, and four men entered. Three of them were obviously muscle, and his heart sank as he saw they carried stun guns—nothing in the way of lethal weapons evident from where he stood.

The man in charge was slender and thirty-something, his black hair slicked back from his oval, seamless face. He wore a stylish suit without the tie, his collar open at the throat. His smile reminded Katzenelenbogen of a hungry lizard staring at a grub.

"I'm glad to see you're feeling better," the man said. "We need to have a little talk."

DETECTIVE SERGEANT David Lau met his informant in a small bar on Connaught Street, near the Macau ferry terminal. The pigeon was a sometime thief and burglar named Jue, aged forty-two or thereabouts, with prison time behind him. He wasn't an oath-bound member of the 14K, but he had served that Triad in the past and had friends in the ranks at different levels. They discussed their business with him now and then, and Jue sorted out the details he could sell to Lau for cash or favors.

He had been tuned in to the violence aimed at Edward Wong since it began, expecting Lau would come to him with questions. They haggled over price for a while, until cash changed hands and Lau agreed to intercede on Jue's behalf in any felony arrest over the next three months, excepting drugs and homicide. Both men had known the rules when they sat down to play.

"You're sure it was a round-eye?" Lau demanded.

"I was told so," Jue replied. "Of course we weren't introduced."

"And when was this?"

"This morning, early. I was coming home from—let us say, a business errand—and I met a friend."

"He's 14K?" Lau asked.

"Since he was old enough to take the oath," Jue replied.

"And still, he told you this?"

"You know me, Sergeant. I heard about Wong's troubles on the street. It was entirely natural for me to ask."

"And you were told...?"

"What I've already said. That they wouldn't be troubled long, since one of those responsible had blundered and was now their prisoner. They were interrogating him, or planned to. He will tell them anything they want to know, in time."

Lau had been working to defeat the Triads since day one of his promotion to detective. Even earlier, when he was still in uniform, Lau had been conscious of their evil influence—the crimes they spawned by peddling drugs, extorting money from their fellow countrymen and operating crooked gambling dens. In terms of simple theft, the Triads looted homes and businesses alike, or dealt with those who did, obtaining merchandise for resale, storing precious information until it could be used to good effect, for blackmail or "persuasion" in the proper areas.

Lau was no vigilante; he didn't believe in picking up a gun to settle problems that were better solved in court...but there were times, he understood, when rules didn't apply. Police around the world made judgment calls like that ten thousand times each day. If it was possible to harm the 14K by helping Mike Belasko to retrieve his friend, Lau felt obliged to do his best. If that made him an ally—or accomplice—of the tall American, then he would have to sort the problem out between his conscience and himself. The brass at city hall already knew what he was doing, most of it. Indeed, it had been their idea.

"You weren't told where they were holding him?" Lau asked.

Jue shook his head. "It would have been too much. I'm not convinced my friend possessed that knowledge, as it was."

"Or who had captured him?" Lau pressed.

"The 14K. That's all I know."

"It isn't much," the sergeant said.

"We have a deal, regardless. Yes?"

"I keep my word. If I find out that you've been holding something back to drive the price up—"

"Please!" Jue's face conveyed a look of wounded innocence. "I have a certain reputation to protect."

"Indeed."

Lau rose and left the bar. He took a deep breath of the harbor's reek to clear his nostrils of the smoke and other smells that filled the bar, exchanging one stench for another.

Such was life.

He checked his watch. Forty minutes remained before he should expect Belasko's call at headquarters. He knew the tall American wouldn't be idle in the meantime. From reports he was receiving, Wong hadn't really improved his situation by capturing the prisoner. If anything, the new round of attacks seemed more intense, an all-out challenge to the hill chief's power.

Would the little information he possessed allow Belasko to retrieve his friend? It seemed unlikely, but stranger things had happened in Lau's world.

"I need to know if he's alive or dead."

Lau thought he knew that much, at least, and he would pass it on. He hoped that it would be enough to bring the hill chief down.

BOLAN HAD the office number memorized, and he peered through the big scope on his Weatherby Mark V while he was tapping out the digits on his compact mobile telephone. Across the street, through lightly tinted glass, he saw the Triad captain break off giving orders to a trio of lieutenants, scowling as he picked up his private line.

"Wei."

"Let's speak English," Bolan said. The face in his cross hairs registered surprise.

"Who is this?"

"Names don't matter, do they? I just called to recommend that you release the one-armed man, unharmed, by one o'clock this afternoon."

His target's eyes blinked once.

"I don't know what you mean."

"Too bad. You never know exactly what might happen, while you're playing dumb."

He laid the telephone aside and swung the rifle several inches to his right. Another face filled the scope, this one a decade younger, studying his master while the older man asked questions into empty air.

A gentle squeeze was all it took, and the .460 Weatherby Magnum kicked against his shoulder like an angry mule, the heavy bullet well downrange by then. It drilled the window cleanly, plowed into the profile filling Bolan's scope and tore the young man's head apart as if someone had stuffed his mouth with cherry bombs.

The bolt worked smoothly, spent brass rattling on the rooftop somewhere to the warrior's right. He had the second shot lined up before his targets knew exactly what was happening. The older man behind the desk had dropped his telephone, ears ringing from the gunshot, spilling over backward, chair and all.

No matter.

He wasn't supposed to die this morning. He was the chosen messenger, and he would carry Bolan's words to Edward Wong.

The other two Chinese were on their feet, presenting Bolan with a better range of targets as he fired a second round. It struck the taller of them in the chest, an inch or so below his heart, and slammed him back against the nearest wall. With a slug that size, it hardly mattered if you missed a vital organ, as it ripped through the abdomen and shredded arteries, unleashing massive blood loss.

Number two was dead before he hit the floor.

And that left one.

He had the final target marked before the young man turned and broke in the direction of the door. It was a clean shot, putting one between his shoulder blades that lifted him completely off his feet and pitched him facefirst into impact with the door he was so desperate to reach.

Enough.

He packed the rifle, retrieved his mobile phone and walked back to the staircase that would take him to the street. His message was delivered, but it wouldn't be the last, by any means. The Executioner wouldn't relent until he knew Wong understood.

And for the moment, bullets talked, while bullshit walked.

15

The telephone had once again become an enemy to Edward Wong. One piece of good news in the past three weeks, and now it seemed as if it were about to blow up in his face. They had one of the round-eyes, and he was being grilled for information, but the others seemed about to go berserk in their attempts to get him back.

The hill chief of the 14K wasn't a man to be intimidated by his enemies. He paid his troops to risk—or even sacrifice—their lives in crisis situations, for the Triad's sake. It troubled him that the attacks were still continuing, but he felt no more sorrow for an individual subordinate who lost his life than if a dog had been run over in the street.

What mattered was the family at large—and Wong himself, as leader and symbolic figurehead. His men knew that when they stood up to take the rambling oaths that bound them to the 14K for life. There was no shortage of young guns to fill the ranks, but Wong's prestige was suffering from the attacks—not only with his troops, but with the Dragon in Macau.

He had to do something soon to remedy the situation, or it might well be too late. Cheung Kuo and his superiors wouldn't hang on forever, waiting for the tide to turn. Their loss was minuscule so far, in terms of personnel, but they had money riding on the line, and Communists were no more understanding when it came to catastrophic losses than your average businessman.

Wong dialed a Hong Kong number from his desk and waited through four rings, speaking briskly when a voice responded on the other end.

"Get Sheng," he said. "I don't care what he's doing! Put him on the telephone at once!"

A moment later Sheng the Torturer was on the line.

"Good morning, sir."

"Has he spoken yet?"

"No, sir. It may require some time."

"I want results, not more excuses! Do you understand?"

"Yes, sir. Of course."

"Then do your job!"

Wong slammed down the telephone receiver with force enough to make his fingers ache. Frustration seethed inside him until he took a breath and held it, both hands clutching the edge of his desk until the knuckles whitened. At last he felt the tension starting to recede—not gone, by any means, but fading to manageable levels.

It would be the end of everything if Wong couldn't maintain his self-control. The Dragon had to have doubts concerning his ability already. How much worse would they become if Wong allowed himself to wallow in self-pity, lose his grip when it was most important for him to maintain control?

They still had time. He trusted Sheng the Torturer to get results. The captive would spill everything he knew, most probably within the next few hours. When he did, their enemies would stand exposed. Wong would only have to send his troops to mop them up.

The victory had been a long time coming, and it wasn't yet safely within his grasp. But it was coming.

Wong could feel it.

And for the first time in three weeks, the hill chief of the 14K allowed himself to smile.

McCARTER SNIFFED his fingers, smelling motor oil though none was visible, and took a towelette from the car's glove compartment. He had nearly finished wiping off his hands when the Mercedes-Benz nosed through the exit of the underground garage, downrange, and turned left into traffic, headed west.

He crumpled up the towelette, dropped it on the floor and pulled into the traffic behind his quarry. The Mercedes had a lead of forty yards, and that was fine for now. The red light on the plastic box that occupied the seat beside him winked in almost perfect tempo with McCarter's pulse.

It had been dicey, creeping into the garage and underneath the Benz to plant the plastique charge against the fuel tank. He was gambling that the owner and his entourage wouldn't show up ahead of time and catch him at his work, and he had won that bet.

So far, so good.

The owner of the Benz was Richard Fang, a top enforcer for the 14K in Hong Kong and Kowloon. Besides the driver, Fang had two young shooters with him, a concession to the climate of the times. And if McCarter's information was correct, he would be headed for the house near Aberdeen, the southwest corner of the island, where he kept a twenty-year-old mistress.

Following the men he meant to kill, McCarter thought of Katz, uncertain whether he was still alive, and felt no pity for the soldiers in the Benz. Whatever happened on the road to Aberdeen, Fang had been asking for it all his life. The others were no better, pledging their allegiance to a criminal brotherhood that preyed upon the weaklings of society for profit, utterly remorseless.

So would his vengeance be, without remorse.

The traffic thinned as they drove out of central Hong Kong, following a highway that would take them past Victoria Peak, looping southward from there to Aberdeen, on the coast facing Ocean Park. There would be even fewer cars once they began the short run south, but it was doubtful they would ever have the highway strictly to themselves. McCarter knew that he would have to choose his moment, key the detonator when he had an opening and minimize the danger to civilian passersby.

He thought about Bolan's contact with the Hong Kong police, wondering if it would yield any useful information to help them find out what had happened to Katz. It was a long shot, granted, but he had to keep his fingers crossed—at least symbolically—while they were trying other angles of attack.

Like squeezing Edward Wong until he popped.

It was the hill chief's bad luck to be managing the 14K when Bolan and his Phoenix Force comrades came to town. Worse yet, if Wong had stolen Katz away from them, a longtime friend and valued member of the team. What Bolan and McCarter had in mind for Wong was bad enough before, but if it came down to a blood feud . . .

The Mercedes-Benz had slowed, following a long curve in the highway. Hanging back as traffic thinned, McCarter wondered if the driver might have spotted him. The same car on their tail from central Hong Kong to the present point would be enough to generate suspicion, maybe call for some evasive action, but the joke was on his enemies in that regard. The detonator on the seat beside him had a one-mile range, and it wasn't dependent on an unobstructed line of sight. The only way for Richard Fang to save himself was if McCarter fell asleep and let the Benz escape.

And that wasn't about to happen.

Not today.

Another fifteen minutes brought them to the clearest stretch of highway yet. There was a produce truck perhaps a quarter mile ahead, a motorcycle running eighty or a hundred yards behind McCarter, nothing visible approaching in the other lane. The Briton palmed the detonator, aimed it at the Benz—although he knew the gesture was unnecessary—and depressed the plastic button with his thumb.

The sleek Mercedes went to hell. McCarter's bomb ripped through its fuel tank, primary and secondary detonations merging into one, a thunderclap that rocked the Phoenix Force warrior's rental car. Another heartbeat, and the Benz was standing on its nose, forward momentum and the shock wave of the blast combining to flip it like a toy. It landed on its roof amid a spreading lake of fire.

McCarter had no cover to preserve. He didn't make a show of pulling over, stepping out and gawking at the twisted, smoking wreckage. Rather, he was quick to put the rental car through a tight U-turn and head back toward central Hong Kong.

Where the action was.

"You ain't seen nothing yet," he muttered to himself, accelerating while the funeral pyre of Richard Fang began to dwindle in his rearview mirror. Smaller. Smaller. Gone.

The war was waiting for him, back on Hong Kong's teeming streets: revenge or rescue, either way.

And he wouldn't have missed it for the world.

Macau

BY NOON the Dragon had begun preparing his defenses. He had trusted Edward Wong up to a point, even relaxed a little when the hill chief told him they had captured one of the adventurers responsible for raising so much hell among his allies in the past weeks. Regardless of that breakthrough, though, and its potential for allowing them to trap the others, Wong and his associates were still the targets of attacks in Hong Kong, losing more men by the hour. Cheung

Kuo suspected that the capture of a hostage might have backfired—it was often so with terrorists, who escalated their attacks from stubborn pride, instead of backing off when they were challenged—and he saw no reason to believe that Wong would be successful, where so many of his field commanders had already failed to stop the enemy.

In which case, the Dragon thought, he would have to do it on his own. He had his own troops in Macau, completely independent of the 14K. They were recruited from the People's Army, members of a crack commando unit, requisitioned for special service to the party and their homeland. They didn't ask questions when the uniforms came off, and they would never think of disobeying orders.

They were perfect.

On the down side, he had only forty soldiers in Macau, the maximum that he could easily conceal in make-work jobs without attracting the unwelcomed notice of authorities. The forty were prepared to leave their mock employment at a moment's notice, and he had already sent out the order, detailing men to watch the ferries and commercial piers. That duty used up half his soldiers, but he could call them back if need be to protect himself.

The Dragon was a man who understood the risks of his profession, who had long ago prepared himself to sacrifice his life, if necessary, for the People's Revolution, but he didn't take death lightly. He had slain too many men himself, or had it done by others, to believe that death was noble—much less neat and clean.

If death was coming to Macau, he meant for it to find his enemies, while he lived on to scheme and fight another day. He would be hatching plots against the West long after these, his momentary adversaries, were reduced to dust and ashes.

Still, he thought, Wong might get lucky. It wasn't impossible. Depending on the number of his enemies, and whether they were gullible enough to take the bait, he still might rub them out.

But if he failed, if it was obvious that Kuo was on his own, the Dragon would be ready. He wouldn't allow himself to be caught napping, unprepared. Whatever happened, he would give his enemies a fight they wouldn't soon forget.

He felt the heat from his superiors increasing, day by day, but they wouldn't recall him from the field at this stage of the game. There was no viable replacement, no one who could step into his shoes and run the operation he had built with Edward Wong. It was a fragile partnership, grown positively brittle in the face of recent pressure, but the hill chief of the 14K was still a man who kept his word...up to a point.

It would be foolish—even suicidal—for the Triad leader to turn traitor on him now, but it wasn't beyond Wong's capability to seek new channels of communication with Beijing behind Kuo's back. The Dragon had his adversaries in the Party, though they made a point of showing a united face in public, and he was aware of several who would gladly steal his grand idea, take credit for its ultimate success...or blame the most convenient dead man if it failed.

Kuo had his faults, but he wasn't naive. The first thing he had learned, when he was still a young man climbing through the party ranks, had been to watch his back. For all the talk of brotherhood, Mao's sacred guiding principles, the commonality of man, he recognized that there were Communists who put their own needs before the people and the Party they were sworn to serve.

Kuo had done the same himself on more than one occasion, and he would again.

Assuming he survived the next few days.

He thought of calling Wong to check on any progress in the past two hours but decided it would be a bad idea. It made no sense to show the gangster he was worried, when they needed strength and courage to preserve them in this time of trial.

He could afford to wait, at least a little while.

And in the meantime he would strengthen his defenses, lay his snares and wait for some rash fool to spring the trap.

His adversaries would make a grave mistake, if they believed the Dragon was incapable of fending for himself. That kind of error got men killed. It happened every day.

The waiting game was one that Kuo had long since learned to play. In fact, he was a master, as his enemies would soon learn to their sorrow.

When the time came, they would wish there was a god above to hear their prayers for mercy, as the Dragon's fiery breath gave them a taste of hell on earth.

THE TELEPHONE RANG three times, starting on a fourth before somebody picked it up. A strong, familiar voice said, "Sergeant Lau."

"Belasko," Bolan told him. "Can you talk?"

"I'll meet you. Fifteen minutes?"

"Fine."

Lau named a restaurant on Chater Road, just south of city hall, and severed the connection. Bolan left the phone booth, walked back to his car and drove six blocks to find a more or less convenient parking space.

The restaurant was small and filling up, still close enough to lunchtime for the lawyers and financial types who might be running late. He got a table near the window, saw Lau coming from across the street and waited while the hostess guided him to Bolan's table. Lau declined a menu, ordered tea and started talking once the waitress had left them.

"I have news, but nothing very helpful, I'm afraid," Lau said.

"I'm listening."

"I spoke to some of my informants. Only one of them knew anything. A member of the 14K told him they have a foreign prisoner. A round-eye."

"Still alive?"

"Supposedly, at two or three o'clock this morning." Lau didn't sound hopeful. "There are no more details. My informant was afraid to ask and thereby make himself conspicuous."

"It's something, anyway."

"If true," Lau said. "We must assume the prisoner to be your friend—it's too much to think the Triads would abduct two white men in a single day—but there is still the time lapse to consider."

He was right, of course. Assuming Katz was bagged as late as 3:00 a.m., it would be going on ten hours now. Allow some time for transportation, waking up the boss and getting orders to proceed, and it was still entirely possible that Katz had been put through the mill by now, wrung dry of information and eliminated. It might not be common knowledge in the gang, much less to hangers-on and marginal police informants. There was no one he could trust, in fact, except the boss of bosses.

Edward Wong.

"I need to find out more," he said.

Lau spread his hands. "There is no more to tell. If I hear anything, of course..."

"I wasn't thinking of your people," Bolan told him, almost talking to himself.

"What, then?"

"I'm betting you don't really want to know."

Lau thought about that for a moment, frowning, sipping at his tea. "The wise thing is for me to walk away," he

said, "and make believe we never met. It's strange, though
how the wisdom sometimes fades with age, instead of mul
tiplying."

"It gets ugly," Bolan said. "If you mix in, it's all one
way. There's nothing I can do to help you with your peo
ple if it blows up in our faces."

"I have worked against the Triads, in one fashion or an
other, since I joined the force," Lau said. "We pick up th
small change from time to time. A ranking officer is pros
ecuted once in a career, if that. For me, so far, there hav
been disappointments, many slips of paper going into file
that I can never use, because the information does no
qualify as evidence. If I retired to write a book, perhaps i
would be useful. Otherwise..."

"There's all the difference in the world between frustra
tion and a shooting war," Bolan said. He was hesitant t
shun an ally who could help him, most especially when
life was riding on the line, but he wouldn't recruit Lau un
der false pretenses.

"You aren't concerned with bringing Edward Wong t
trial, am I correct?" Lau asked.

"It never crossed my mind."

"There will be no reports on file...at least where offi
cers of my department would have access to them?"

"No."

Lau smiled. "Then all I truly have to fear is bein
killed."

The detective's smile was infectious. "You consider tha
a small thing?" Bolan asked him.

"No," Lau said, "but sometimes it's worth the risk, i
something good can be accomplished."

"To be honest with you," Bolan replied, "I have mor
use for information than an extra gun."

"And if you could have both?"

"Right now," he said, "I wouldn't turn it down."

"It's settled then. I have more inquiries to make, but frankly I'm not convinced they'll be helpful. In the meantime—" he produced a business card and handed it across to Bolan "—if you find out where your friend is being held, the second number is my private telephone at home. There may be places where a badge can open doors more easily than guns."

"Before you go," Bolan said, taking out a pen and scribbling numbers on a scrap of paper napkin, "this number is for my mobile phone."

Lau read the number, memorized it, then produced a match and watched it burn in the ashtray, between them. "Done," he stated, and rose to leave.

"Be careful, okay?" Bolan said.

"I would give the same advice to you," Lau replied, "but something tells me safety goes against your nature."

Bolan watched him go, paid off the tab and left the restaurant when Lau was out of sight. It was a short walk to his car, and the Executioner used the time to think about what he had learned from the detective. Nothing much, except the possibility that Katz was still alive.

His next step, Bolan thought, would be to find out from the horse's mouth.

THE CHAIR WAS WOODEN and straight-backed, with its heavy legs set far enough apart that Katzenelenbogen couldn't rock it—even when he strained with all his might against the leather straps that held him fast. The straps themselves, like thick brown belts, were buckled tight around his chest, waist and limbs. His head hung forward, chin on chest, with perspiration dripping from his face into his lap.

"You are a stubborn man," the Chinese torturer remarked. His thin voice seemed to come from miles away. "I can admire that, honestly, but we are short of time."

Katz shook his head to clear it, instantly regretting the exertion. The explosive pain behind his eyes was different from the raw, burned places on his naked body. Somehow it seemed cumulative. Each new jolt of electricity ran through his nerve synapses to his brain and made his skull throb as if it might burst.

The lame attempt to overcome his captors had been fruitless. Katz had broken one man's nose, or thought he had, before the stun guns put him down and out. When he regained his senses, Katz was buckled in the chair and helpless.

So far he had told them nothing—didn't *think* he had, at least, although things got a little hazy after they applied the stun guns half a dozen times to different portions of his body. He was hoarse from screaming, had made no effort to restrain himself from making noise. Pride had no part in his consideration at the moment, and if he should lose his voice, so much the better. It would keep him from responding to their questions when his will snapped—as he knew it had to before much longer.

"Let's start from the beginning, shall we?" his torturer asked.

"Go fuck yourself," Katz rasped, and let his chin fall back onto his chest.

"Such language from a dying man. Are you not worried that your God will be offended?"

Katz made no reply to that. He heard the stun gun crackle as his captor tested it, made sure the battery hadn't run down too far to do its job.

"From the beginning, then. Who sent you here? Who are you working for?"

"United Garbage Handlers," Katz replied. "I'm taking out the trash."

He felt the kiss of the electrodes, the metal cold against his skin, before the pain struck him in waves, exploding from the point of contact like a miniearthquake in his flesh.

And Katz put everything he had into the scream.

WONG'S PRIVATE NUMBER wasn't difficult to learn. Simplicity itself, in fact, with help from David Lau. A quick word with the afternoon shift supervisor at the telephone exchange, and Bolan was in business. All he needed, then, was someone to assist in presentation of his case.

It didn't matter who, as long as he was a sworn member of the 14K. In the end, he wound up with a loan shark named Chang Hu, whom Bolan intercepted on his way to roust a tailor, six blocks from the U.S. Consulate. A glimpse of Bolan's pistol got him in the car, and a sharp tap on the skull put him under while they drove.

It made no difference where he parked, as long as they were undisturbed. He chose a narrow access road beside a warehouse that was under renovation, with generators, drills and metal-cutting saws providing background noise. He dragged out the loan shark and twisted both ears like the tuning knobs on an old-fashioned TV set until the pain brought him around.

"Do you speak English?"

"Yes."

He palmed the mobile telephone. "I'm calling Edward Wong, your hill chief. When I hand the telephone to you, identify yourself, say anything that comes to mind. Okay?"

The gangster was confused but nodded, wincing as the motion sent a bolt of fresh pain through his skull. He stood and watched as Bolan tapped the number out and waited through two rings, until someone answered in Chinese.

"I need to speak with Edward Wong," Bolan said, trusting that a man assigned to answer telephones would have at least a working knowledge of the English language. "You can tell him it's the round-eye who's been chasing him around the city since last night."

"Wait, please."

He counted fifty seconds until Wong came on the line, and he smiled at the idea of someone working on a trace.

"Hello," Wong said, "who's this?"

"You wouldn't recognize my name," Bolan replied, "but I've been examining your operations for more than two weeks now. Starting off in San Francisco."

"I was hoping we might have a chance to speak."

"I know you're busy," Bolan went on, "and I've still got a ton of things to do, so here's the deal. You grabbed a friend of mine this morning, and I want him back alive. Until that happens, anything that went down before is small potatoes. Do you follow me?"

"A threat?" Wong's tone was mocking. "If you think—"

"I've got somebody here who wants to say hello," Bolan said, interrupting him.

With that, he gave Hu the telephone and nodded. The man began to speak Cantonese, but Bolan waited only long enough to hear his name pronounced before he drew his Browning autoloader from its shoulder rig and shot the loan shark in the face at point-blank range.

The Browning had no silencer, its echo joining the construction sounds that issued from next door. He caught the telephone as it was falling, listened briefly to the sound of breathing on the other end before he spoke again.

"That's one more down," Bolan said. "I assume this loser meant as much to you as any of your soldiers, which is nothing, but I picked him up to make a point. Until my friend is safe and sound, you can expect one nonstop holiday in hell."

"And if I grant your wish, what then?" Wong asked.

"We talk," the soldier stated, lying through his teeth.

"Perhaps we should arrange a meeting, then," the hill chief said.

To which the Executioner replied, "I'm listening."

16

Macau

The Dragon could have easily rejected Wong's suggestion that the enemy be slaughtered in Macau, rather than Hong Kong, but he went along for several reasons. First, it would impress his masters if the plan appeared to spring from Cheung Kuo's brain, instead of Edward Wong's. An ambush in Macau would let him supervise, play any role he liked, while making sure Wong's people didn't let the sharks slip through their net again. Such personal concerns aside, there had been ample violence on the streets of Hong Kong as it was, and anything that drew the heat away, allowed their other operations to proceed without official scrutiny, was good for business.

Accordingly the Dragon had decided he would oversee the ambush personally. Wong would join him, standing by to take the blame if anything went wrong, disposable in an emergency. If all went according to their plan, the troubling business should be settled in an hour's time and they could all get back to normal operations.

Kuo no longer cared who was responsible for the attacks. It was enough for him to know that the Americans had been involved. His future efforts to destroy their decadent society would be more energetic than before, propelled as much by private anger as by dedication to the cause.

A site had been selected on the waterfront, with Wong pretending to agree with the demand to free his round-eyed prisoner. The man was still alive by pure dumb luck, but he wouldn't last long once his compatriots arrived.

A clean sweep was in order, and the Dragon meant to see it through, even if he was forced to take a gun and do the job himself. In fact, he was armed when he joined his soldiers. He would leave the fighting to subordinates if possible, but Kuo wasn't afraid to get his own hands bloody if the situation should require it.

Driving toward the Inner Harbor waterfront, Kuo reached inside his jacket to extract the Skorpion machine pistol he carried there in an elaborate shoulder harness. It was fully loaded, with a live round in the chamber and the safety on, in case he had to draw and fire in haste. It was unlikely, Kuo told himself, but it was also best to be prepared.

When he was satisfied, he put the gun away and concentrated on his plans. In a mere two hours his problems would be over.

BOLAN KNEW THEY WOULD be waiting for him; nothing else made any sense. Despite the beating Wong had taken, he wasn't about to crumble with a phone call, much less when he had to know there was small chance of Bolan backing off once Katzenelenbogen was returned. They had a death game going, and it would be played out to the end. It didn't take a genius to decide that using Katz for bait could be a better ploy than grilling him for information on the side.

The Executioner had no way of knowing whether he was still alive, but it had almost ceased to matter. Bolan still intended to retrieve his friend, if there was any chance at all, but he would have to deal with Wong and company, whatever happened.

And there was the matter of a certain Dragon to consider, too.

The word had come from David Lau about the hill chief's contact in Macau. A mainland diplomat, he called himself, but Cheung Kuo was more than that—a great deal more. Hong Kong police had linked his name to acts of sabotage and covert ops that spanned the past five years. On more than one occasion, they had tried to infiltrate his network, but their agents always wound up dead, the last one toasted with a flamethrower the same night he was scheduled to extract himself and present to his bosses sufficient evidence to win indictments.

Kuo himself would be untouchable—the diplomatic thing—but they could lodge a protest in the months remaining, maybe have him called back to Beijing just long enough to leave the ChiCom apparatus in confusion.

But it hadn't worked. Their man—like those before him—was another "unsolved" homicide statistic, and the game went on.

Until tonight.

He smelled the trap, approaching from the pier where he had tied the rented speedboat. Spotters would be watching for him at the ferry terminals, primarily, and while it never crossed his mind that he could slip into Macau unnoticed by the enemy, each moment gained was something in his favor. And McCarter should be well in place by now.

The night was warm, but Bolan wore a lightweight overcoat, regardless. It was mandatory, with the hardware he was carrying: an Uzi and the Browning, half a dozen extra magazines for each, four frag grenades and one smoke canister. McCarter had the heavy-duty stuff, if he found a stand and had a chance to use it.

Bolan recognized the pier Wong had selected for the meet. There were no fishermen around this time of night. They had the whole place to themselves. One limo stood at

center stage as he approached, three Triad soldiers lounging against one side. Wong wasn't visible, though he had
made it clear he would be coming to the meet himself.
Likewise, no sign of Katz, but he should be inside the car,
assuming he was even here.

Or maybe in the trunk.

How better to transport a corpse?

To Bolan's left, some twenty yards inland, a row of
warehouses stood dark against the city lights. The harbor
was off to his right, the vast Pacific stretching on forever.
It was relatively open on the pier, but there were places
where a rifle company could hide and still be close enough
to spring a trap once he walked into it.

The Executioner drew back the right side of his raincoat
to free the Uzi, one hand on its pistol grip as he advanced.
When he had reached the pier, with another sixty feet between himself and the black limousine, he heard the sound
of racing engines from behind and turned to see more vehicles emerging from the shadows cloaking the warehouses.

The trap was relatively obvious, straightforward, no less
deadly for its evident simplicity. And he was ready for
them.

He raised the submachine gun, finger on its trigger, as he
spun to face the gunners standing by the limousine.

WONG CURSED A BLUE STREAK when he saw that it was only
one man, come to save his comrade. He had been expecting at least three or four, and apprehension seized him,
battened on the thought that he was being tricked, somehow, the trap reversed so that he snared himself.

In the few seconds that remained, before he had to give
the signal to his troops, Wong thought about the sketchy
field reports, descriptions and the like, that he had gath-

ered from survivors of his family in North America, Europe, Rangoon and Bangkok.

Could it be that only two men were responsible for all the headaches he had suffered in the past few weeks? Of course, there would be someone else behind them, pulling the important strings, but in a way it made good sense to field the smallest force available. Why send a dozen men to get in one another's way and make things difficult, when one or two could carry out a mission more effectively?

Wong's next sensation was a rush of disappointment—had he pulled out all the stops to bag *one man?*—but then he thought of what this man and his companion had already done in Hong Kong. He thought about the other target cities, where his family lay in smoking ruins, and Wong told himself the tall round-eye had much to answer for.

He grabbed the walkie-talkie, thumbed the button and barked instructions to his soldiers who waited in the other car beyond his view. At the same moment, Wong leaned forward, slapped his driver on the shoulder and their vehicle leaped forward, rubber smoking on the pavement.

They were closing on the target, speeding closer, when the left-front tire exploded and Wong's car began to swerve. Before the hill chief knew it, his whole world was upside down.

McCARTER SQUEEZED the Barrett Fifty's trigger and felt the heavy weapon slam against his shoulder. He peered through the telescopic sight to register a hit. The nearer of the two attack cars swerved, tipped over on its side and wound up on its roof, three good tires spinning in the air, while number four flapped shreds of rubber like a giant reel of broken film.

He had been lying on the warehouse roof for three full hours, waiting for their adversaries to arrive, for the Executioner to show himself and spring the trap. McCarter was the ace up Bolan's sleeve, the Barrett Fifty adding muscle to what otherwise could easily have been a suicidal ploy.

And it might still turn out that way, McCarter thought, but he was trimming the odds. He swung the muzzle of his weapon through a shallow arc and found the second car as it was screeching to a halt. Before the doors flew open, he was sighting on the driver's window, squeezing off a second round that burst the tinted glass as if a sledgehammer had been applied. He didn't see the driver sprawl across his seat, but there was evident confusion as the troops piled out with guns in hand.

The Briton chose one man and slammed an armor-piercing round into his chest. The Chinese gunner vaulted over backward, twitching on the pavement while a couple of his friends stood gaping, still uncertain where the hostile fire was coming from.

By that time, Bolan was unloading on the others with his Uzi, but the odds were still at nine or ten to one against him, more troops leaping from the limousine that had been waiting for him on the pier when he arrived. A couple of the doors were open on that vehicle, as well, and battered-looking troops were crawling out—one with a crimson smear across his face, another lurching when he tried to stand, then clutching at his head.

McCarter framed the gunman's twisted features in his telescopic sight and stroked the Barrett's trigger, watching as the target's skull was vaporized. The body staggered backward three short steps before it slumped against the car and moved no more.

He still had half a dozen rounds left in the Barrett's magazine, but he had to take it easy on the limousine that occupied the pier. For all he knew, Katz might be in the car, and armor-piercing rounds weren't smart bombs; they had no idea of who was standing in their way when they drilled metal, seeking flesh and bone.

McCarter swung back toward the second car, already wondering how long he could harass Wong's soldiers without someone spotting him and returning fire. He had the high ground, granted, but a pincers movement could surround him if they had sufficient numbers to pull it off.

As if in answer to his thoughts, McCarter heard more vehicles approaching, coming from his right. He lifted off the Barrett's scope and peered in that direction, checking the scene, afraid that the police had somehow tumbled to the action and responded with unusual alacrity.

But it was even worse.

Another pair of crew wagons were racing toward the pier, guns bristling from the open windows, reinforcements closing in to tip the scales.

"God*damn* it!"

There was nothing he could do but hold his ground and fight.

Determined to succeed or die in the attempt, McCarter brought his gun around and bent back to the eyepiece of his scope.

"All right, you bastards, come and get it!"

IT WAS OBVIOUS to Cheung Kuo that Edward Wong couldn't control the situation. With the ambush barely seconds old, one of his vehicles had been disabled, while his men were being cut down left and right. The trap was flawed, but it could still be salvaged, with a touch of Dragon's fire.

He drew the Skorpion and thumbed off the safety. The second car, behind him, held another seven gunners, for a total of fifteen in all. One man—or more, if he had someone sniping from the sidelines—would be swiftly overwhelmed and taken down.

Or so he thought.

He changed his mind when something struck the left side of the car with a resounding clang, as if a baseball bat had slammed against the driver's door. The wheelman gave a strangled cry and arched his back, released the steering wheel and started groping for the place where he was wounded. With his foot off the accelerator, they began to lose momentum, slowing.

A sniper on the left! But where? One of the Dragon's soldiers was already firing in that direction through his window, but it was a wasted effort. He couldn't have seen the muzzle-flash, when all eyes had been focused on the pier in front of them before the bullet struck.

And what a bullet it had to be! What kind of weapons were they facing here? What kind of men were these?

He glanced back at the tail car and saw it pulling abreast of his, but on the right-hand side, so that Kuo's vehicle would block the unseen sniper's fire. It was a sound maneuver on the driver's part, but Kuo wished the man was more concerned with covering his master than himself.

In front of him, one of his soldiers reached around the wounded driver, gripped the steering wheel and slammed his own foot on the accelerator to prevent the car from stalling out. The vehicle surged forward at once, closing on the pier where muzzle-flashes lit the night, a pair of gunmen on Kuo's left still firing toward the line of darkened warehouses beyond.

Was that a wink of gunfire on the center rooftop, answering their fire? The Dragon barely had a chance to pose that question in his mind before a heavy bullet struck the nearest of his soldiers, ripping through his upper torso, spraying blood around the inside of the car before it shattered the rear window.

Kuo ducked below the sniper's line of sight, but knew that wasn't enough to save him if his gun could fire through

armor-plated steel. Salvation lay in speed, and they had almost reached the point where they would have to stop, pile
out and join the fight.

The Dragon wished he could remember how to pray.

A SHORT BURST from the Uzi dropped a second gunner to
his knees, his hands clasped across a bloody midriff as he
toppled forward on his face. Two down, and Bolan left the
reinforcements to McCarter for the moment, concentrating on the shooters who were leaping from the limousine to
challenge him.

He counted four, plus one of the originals still on his feet
and circling around behind the limousine for cover. That
should be the lot of them, unless Wong had his men wedged
in the vehicle like circus clowns inside a funny car. A couple of them were already firing as they hit the pavement.
Bolan flattened himself against the deck and tracked with
the Uzi, raking them with automatic fire.

He cut one gunner's legs from under him and slammed
him back against the limo, twitching as he fell across the
Uzi's line of fire. The second hasty shooter caught a
3-round burst above the belt line, doubling over as the bullets ripped his flesh, the last rounds from his automatic
weapon chewing up the deck around his feet.

The surviving gunners were behind the limo now, and
momentarily concealed. A backward glance showed Bolan
four cars on the waterfront, one rolled over on its roof, the
others in a sloppy semicircle, cutting off retreat. Beyond
them, from the rooftop of a warehouse fifty yards away, the
flash and thunder of McCarter's cannon told the Executioner that he wasn't alone.

But where was Katz? Inside the limo? In the trunk? Had
he been killed and dumped somewhere before the rendezvous?

There was only one way to find out.

He couldn't risk a frag grenade if Katz was in the limousine, so Bolan palmed the round smoke canister and yanked its pin, tossing the smoker overhand before his adversaries mastered their initial shock and came out shooting. It bounced atop the limo's roof, then fell among them, hissing, giving off a cloud of dense white smoke.

They panicked, unfamiliar with grenades or simply taken by surprise. The Executioner was ready for them when they burst from cover, two around the rear end of the car and one around the front.

He took the twosome first, a raking burst that dropped them both together, arms and legs tangled up in death. From there, he swung to face the solitary gunner who came charging at him, firing blindly through the smoke. His rounds were high, more danger to the reinforcements lined up on the dock than to his target. Bolan squeezed off a short burst to the chest that lifted the man completely off his feet and dropped him on his back.

It was time to check the limousine before his luck ran out. The warrior vaulted to his feet and rushed the car, heard guns begin to sputter on his flank when he was almost there.

He reached the car, wrenched one door open in a rush and flung himself inside.

IT SEEMED TO KATZ that he was struggling upward from the depths of an abysmal sea, lungs bursting, with the surface far above his head. The darkness faded by degrees, too slowly for his straining eyes. The throbbing of his own pulse in his ears was loud enough to be mistaken for the sound of gunfire, and . . . what was it?

How could he smell smoke when he was underwater, drowning?

Someone grasped his arm and shook him roughly. Had the lifeguard come in after him? Katz sputtered, thrashing, but his arms were bound behind him, making it impossible for him to swim.

His eyes snapped open, focusing on Bolan's face. A knife blade, cool against his skin, severed the ropes that bound him. Katzenelenbogen struggled upright, knocking knees with Bolan as he huddled on a jump seat in the limousine. Outside, another burst of automatic gunfire rattled on the car like leaden rain.

"Are you all right?" Bolan asked.

"Better," Katz replied. He wore a T-shirt and a too-small pair of denim jeans that bound him in the crotch, but even with his throbbing skull and the pain of contact burns around his groin and torso, Katz felt better than he had since he was captured by the enemy.

"We need to make a move," Bolan said, nodding toward the line of cars and gunmen fifty feet away, "before those guys get lucky or bring up the big guns."

"Right."

The Executioner produced a Browning automatic from his shoulder rig and handed it to Katz, with two spare magazines. "When we get outside, you may find something better."

"Let's get to it, then."

They bailed out through the driver's side to keep the limo in between themselves and those who sought to kill them, Bolan going first since he had two good hands. Katz left the limo in a crouch, his nostrils flaring with the reek of cordite, popping up to fire a first, experimental shot in the direction of his enemies.

The Browning felt good in his fist. Even if they killed him now, at least he had a chance to go down fighting, not trussed up like someone's Christmas turkey.

There was no good way to die, but some were preferable to others. Any warrior might prefer to die in bed, asleep, at ninety years of age, but few would welcome execution, like a criminal, when there was still a chance to take some of their adversaries with them, going down with all guns blazing to the end.

Katz hoped that he could find the man called Sheng, his torturer, but any member of the Triad would suffice for now. His heart and mind were set on playing catch-up while he still had time.

He was alive and free, and that was all that mattered now. Whatever followed was his destiny, and he would take it as it came.

THE DRAGON CAUGHT a glimpse of Edward Wong, disheveled, bleeding from a cut along his hairline, limping as he tried to put the battleground behind him. Wong saw the late arrivals and veered in their direction from the capsized car in which he had been riding moments earlier. Behind him, members of his hit team were unloading at the limo on the pier, while two round-eyes crouched behind it, steadily returning fire. Away to Kuo's left, the rooftop sniper still chose targets, the reports of his impressive weapon rolling out like thunderclaps across the waterfront.

How could everything have gone so wrong in an instant, when the plan was laid so carefully, their numbers calculated to destroy the enemy?

It had to be Wong's fault. The Dragon could admit no other answer to the questions that bedeviled him. Wong had repeated his mistake of underestimating total strangers, brought a score of soldiers with him when it should have been three dozen, maybe more. Had he been counting on the Dragon's reinforcements to make up his shortage? Did he give the problem any thought at all?

They weren't defeated yet, of course, but time was on the side of their opponents. A few more minutes, at the most, and he would hear the sound of sirens drawing closer, bringing guns and uniforms to ruin everything. Cheung Kuo wasn't afraid of being jailed—his diplomatic pass would see him through that difficulty—but exposure of his criminal behavior in Macau would make him useless. He would be recalled, interrogated in Beijing, and the embarrassment he brought upon his masters would require some drastic punishment.

He had to escape, even if it meant his enemies were left at large. A wise commander knew when he should cut his losses and retreat, instead of wasting time and lives in the pursuit of an objective he couldn't obtain.

Before he left, though, Kuo had business to complete with the leader of the 14K.

He waved a hand at Wong, beheld the hill chief veering toward him on unsteady legs. The Triad boss looked anything but regal at the moment, bleeding from his scalp wound, lurching like a drunkard as he made his way across the asphalt. Kuo was disgusted by the spectacle, unable to express his ultimate contempt in words.

Wong slumped beside him, under cover of the Dragon's car. "We must not stay here," he began, words hissing through his teeth as he sat, panting like a winded dog. "Police will be here soon. My men . . ."

The pistol pressed against his forehead made Wong lose his train of thought. He gaped at Kuo, unable or unwilling to believe the message written on the Dragon's face.

"You've failed me for the last time, Edward. I will have no end of trouble over this night's work."

"It's not my fault!" Wong cried. "I—"

The explosive impact of a bullet fired at skin-touch range slammed Wong's head back against the car with force enough to dent the fender. Blood and brains clung to the limo's paint job as his body toppled over sideways, going limp.

The members of the 14K could choose themselves another hill chief when they had the time. Wong was a casualty of war, another victim of the round-eyes.

Kuo called out to his soldiers, shouting to be heard above the sound of gunfire, snapping orders at them. First one, then another, stopped firing at the enemy and moved to help him back inside the car. A driver was about to slide behind the wheel, when he lurched forward, coughing blood from ruptured lungs, the echo of a distant gunshot coming seconds afterward.

The rooftop sniper!

"Get in the car!" Kuo shouted. "Take the wheel!"

Another of his men was moving to obey when he exploded, fragments of his skull and spongy brain erupting from the wet stump of his neck. Momentum stretched his headless body across the driver's seat, and Kuo's two surviving men took off running like a pair of frightened children, deaf to his commands.

The Dragon had no choice. He cursed and followed, sprinting through the darkness like a thief looking for a place to hide.

MCCARTER FED the Barrett Fifty with a brand-new magazine and swung back toward the line of gunners who had Katz and Bolan cornered on the pier. He could see six men, their backs turned toward him, none apparently aware of grim death waiting on their blind side.

Six for six.

He worked his way from left to right, one round per soldier, forced to hesitate a beat or two between the shots and let his weapon find its mark. McCarter had the fourth man in his cross hairs when they figured out exactly what was happening and bolted, fleeing for their lives.

Out on the pier, his comrades opened up in unison as targets were presented to them, Bolan with his Uzi, Katzenelenbogen with a pistol. There was no great trick to dropping adversaries on the run, and it was done in seconds flat.

McCarter swung back toward the runners who had broken from the car off to his right, but they were gone. Three men . . . or was it four?

He cursed and grabbed the walkie-talkie on his belt, reaching out to Bolan with the news.

"I'M GOING AFTER THEM," Bolan said, switching off before McCarter had a chance to argue with him. There were bodies scattered on the pier and across the parking lot, most of them dead, a few still moving.

Katz would have to finish mopping up if he was able. Bolan had already seen enough to know the Kuo wasn't among the dead. If there was any chance at all to bring him down before he slipped away, it would be worth the added risk.

He ran in the direction indicated by McCarter, slipping into shadows as he reached the nearest warehouse, pausing with his ears alert to any sound of running footsteps. Off to his left and somewhere in the shadows up ahead, there came a scuffling sound.

He followed and heard two voices arguing angrily in Cantonese. A shot rang out, immediately followed by two more, and Bolan homed in on the sounds of gunfire, leading with the Uzi as he ran.

The Executioner wound up in a kind of alley, between two warehouses positioned back-to-back. A row of large garbage containers blocked the other end, preventing access—or escape—in that direction. On the ground in front of him, two bodies sprawled in awkward attitudes of death. A third man, well downrange, was struggling to scale the center garbage bin, perched upon its lip now, ready for a leap across the stinking mounds of trash that might take him clear of danger.

"Freeze!"

The sound of Bolan's voice reached out to sting his adversary like a whiplash. Glancing across his shoulder, the Chinese couldn't believe his eyes. The face, illuminated by a floodlight on the warehouse to his left, was that of Cheung Kuo.

His passport photos didn't do him justice, Bolan thought. They missed the cunning in his eyes, which even panic couldn't wipe away. The pistol in Kuo's right hand started inching around, seeking another human target.

There was nothing to discuss, no point in dragging out the moment. Bolan had identified his target, and the rest came down to action—do or die.

He held down the Uzi's trigger and let it do his talking for him, hosing Kuo with fifteen parabellum rounds from thirty feet away. The Dragon shivered, lost his footing and vaulted backward into mounds of garbage, sprawling there with arms outflung, as if he sought to spread his wings and fly.

But he wouldn't be going anywhere this time, until the garbage men arrived to carry him away.

All done, at last.

The Executioner turned and went to find his friends.

EPILOGUE

Stony Man Farm

"You're sure that's what you want to do?" McCarter asked.

"I'm sure," Katz answered with a solemn nod. "I almost blew the game this time, and more than once. You know I'm right."

A full day had passed since they got back from Macau, and they were gathered in the War Room, underneath a not-so-average farmhouse that looked absolutely normal from the air. Each person present was familiar with the room, and with the atmosphere of tension that enveloped it. But this was different, somehow. They were used to hearing sentences pronounced before a mission, not when it was done.

McCarter frowned, seemed on the point of arguing, but slumped back in his chair. Across the table, Bolan glanced from Katz to Hal Brognola, at the table's head, and back again, considering his words before he spoke.

"It's your decision," he began, "but you'll be missed."

"Not necessarily," Barbara Price said.

All eyes turned toward the woman who served as mission controller at the Farm. She studied each face in its turn before she said, "We've worked out a solution that should fly with all concerned, I think."

"Which is?" McCarter sounded skeptical.

"We've always been shorthanded here," she said. "You know the way techs come and go. It wouldn't hurt to have another hand around the place, full-time. Someone with field experience, that is."

"Desk work?" This time the question came from Katz, who sounded every bit as dubious as McCarter.

"Depends on how you look at it," Brognola said. "If you're concerned about the fieldwork, this could be a decent compromise. Alternatively, there's the pension. You could shop around for something in security. Go back to Israel . . ."

"I have nothing there," Katz told the room at large. Another moment passed before he said, "I'll think about it."

"Fair enough," Brognola said, and turned toward Bolan.

"We're still getting echoes from Macau and Hong Kong. You left them quite a mess back there."

"Beijing?"

"They don't have much to say these days. Cheung Kuo was an embarrassment, but they're inclined to take the line that he was acting on his own. Some kind of rogue without official sanction."

"From Red China? That'll be the day." McCarter's tone was scornful now.

"Nobody's buying it outside Beijing," Brognola stated, "but that's beside the point. You shut them down. It won't prevent them starting up again, we all know that, but they'll think twice. And they'll remember what it cost them, too."

"That's something, anyway," Bolan said.

"Too bloody right," McCarter added. "It tells them who their betters are."

"You think so?" Bolan asked.

The rangy Briton considered it, then shrugged. "Well, better shots, at least."

It took a heartbeat, then the laughter started with Barbara Price and made its way around the table.

And it felt good to laugh, this time. The anger, pain and wet work would be waiting for them come tomorrow, and the next day, and the next. But everybody needed a break from time to time.

The Executioner sat back and let himself relax, gave up trying to think when he had last felt so at ease.

It didn't matter, anyway.

This day was all he had, all he could count on.

And tomorrow would take care of itself.

With terror at home and a nuclear nightmare, Stony Man is the President's last hope

STONY MAN™ 24
BIRD OF PREY

At Stony Man Farm in Virginia, world trouble spots are monitored around the clock. And when watch-and-wait tactics aren't enough, the elite field teams go behind the lines—and beyond the law.

Available in September at your favorite retail outlet.

**Don't miss out on the action in these titles featuring
THE EXECUTIONER®, and STONY MAN™!**

SuperBolan

#61445	SHOWDOWN	$4.99 U.S.	☐
		$5.50 CAN.	☐
#61446	PRECISION KILL	$4.99 U.S.	☐
		$5.50 CAN.	☐
#61447	JUNGLE LAW	$4.99 U.S.	☐
		$5.50 CAN.	☐
#61448	DEAD CENTER	$5.50 U.S.	☐
		$6.50 CAN.	☐

Stony Man™

#61904	TERMS OF SURVIVAL	$4.99 U.S.	☐
		$5.50 CAN.	☐
#61905	SATAN'S THRUST	$4.99 U.S.	☐
		$5.50 CAN.	☐
#61906	SUNFLASH	$5.50 U.S.	☐
		$6.50 CAN.	☐
#61907	THE PERISHING GAME	$5.50 U.S.	☐
		$6.50 CAN.	☐

(limited quantities available on certain titles)

TOTAL AMOUNT	$
POSTAGE & HANDLING	$
($1.00 for one book, 50¢ for each additional)	
APPLICABLE TAXES*	$_____
TOTAL PAYABLE	$_____
(check or money order—please do not send cash)	

To order, complete this form and send it, along with a check or money order for the total above, payable to Gold Eagle Books, to: **In the U.S.:** 3010 Walden Avenue, P.O. Box 9077, Buffalo, NY 14269-9077; **In Canada:** P.O. Box 636, Fort Erie, Ontario, L2A 5X3.

Name:_____

Address:_____ City:_____

State/Prov.:_____ Zip/Postal Code: _____

*New York residents remit applicable sales taxes.
 Canadian residents remit applicable GST and provincial taxes.

GEBACK15A

**Blazing a perilous trail through
the heart of darkness**

JAMES AXLER

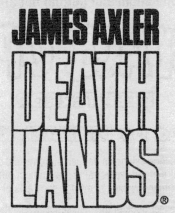

DEATH
LANDS ®

Eclipse at Noon

The nuclear exchange that ripped apart the world destroyed a way
of life thousands of years in the making. Now, generations after the
nuclear blight, Ryan Cawdor and his band of warrior survivalists
try to reclaim the hostile land, led by an undimmed vision of a
better future.

It's winner take all in the Deathlands.

**American hostages abroad have
one chance of getting out alive**

BLACK OPS #3

DEEP TERROR

created by MICHAEL KASNER

Americans are increasingly in danger, at home and abroad. Created
by an elite cadre of red-tape-cutting government officials, the
Black Ops commandos exist to avenge such acts of terror.

The postal system branches out...from
first-class to *first-class* terror

Destroyer

#104 Angry White Mailmen

Created by
WARREN MURPHY
and RICHARD SAPIR

Hell is being hand-delivered in a rash of federal bombings
and random massacres by postal employees across the
nation. And CURE's Dr. Harold Smith sends Remo and
Chiun to root out the cause.

Look for it in October, wherever Gold Eagle books are sold.

**Don't miss out on the action in these titles featuring
THE EXECUTIONER®, and STONY MAN™!**

The Red Dragon Trilogy

#64210	FIRE LASH	$3.75 U.S.	☐
		$4.25 CAN.	☐
#64211	STEEL CLAWS	$3.75 U.S.	☐
		$4.25 CAN.	☐
#64212	RIDE THE BEAST	$3.75 U.S.	☐
		$4.25 CAN.	☐

The Executioner®

#64204	RESCUE RUN	$3.50 U.S.	☐
		$3.99 CAN.	☐
#64205	HELL ROAD	$3.50 U.S.	☐
		$3.99 CAN.	☐
#64206	HUNTING CRY	$3.75 U.S.	☐
		$4.25 CAN.	☐
#64207	FREEDOM STRIKE	$3.75 U.S.	☐
		$4.25 CAN.	☐
#64208	DEATH WHISPER	$3.75 U.S.	☐
		$4.25 CAN.	☐
#64209	ASIAN CRUCIBLE	$3.75 U.S.	☐
		$4.25 CAN.	☐

(limited quantities available on certain titles)

TOTAL AMOUNT	$
POSTAGE & HANDLING	$
($1.00 for one book, 50¢ for each additional)	
APPLICABLE TAXES*	$_____
TOTAL PAYABLE	$_____
(check or money order—please do not send cash)	

To order, complete this form and send it, along with a check or money order for the total above, payable to Gold Eagle Books, to: **In the U.S.:** 3010 Walden Avenue, P.O. Box 9077, Buffalo, NY 14269-9077; **In Canada:** P.O. Box 636, Fort Erie, Ontario, L2A 5X3.

Name:_____

Address:_____ City:_____

State/Prov.:_____ Zip/Postal Code: _____

*New York residents remit applicable sales taxes.
 Canadian residents remit applicable GST and provincial taxes.

GEBACK15